NEARLY
NERO

NEARLY NERO

The Adventures of Claudius Lyon,
the Man Who Would Be Wolfe

LOREN D. ESTLEMAN

Tyrus Books
New York London Toronto Sydney New Delhi

TYRUS BOOKS

Tyrus Books
An Imprint of Simon & Schuster, Inc.
1230 Avenue of the Americas
New York, NY 10020

First Tyrus Books hardcover edition MAY 2017

TYRUS BOOKS and colophon are trademarks of Simon and Schuster.

For information about special discounts for bulk purchases, please contact Simon & Schuster Special Sales at 1-866-506-1949 or business@simonandschuster.com.

The Simon & Schuster Speakers Bureau can bring authors to your live event. For more information or to book an event contact the Simon & Schuster Speakers Bureau at 1-866-248-3049 or visit our website at www.simonspeakers.com.

Interior design by Colleen Cunningham

Manufactured in the United States of America

10 9 8 7 6 5 4 3 2 1

Library of Congress Cataloging-in-Publication Data
Estleman, Loren D., author.
Nearly Nero / Loren D. Estleman.
New York, NY: Tyrus Books, 2017.
LCCN 2016053678 (print) | LCCN 2017001015 (ebook) | ISBN 9781507203279 (hc) | ISBN 9781507203286 (ebook)
BISAC: FICTION / Mystery & Detective / General. | FICTION / Mystery & Detective / Short Stories.
LCC PS3555.S84 A6 2017 (print) | LCC PS3555.S84 (ebook) | DDC 813/.54--dc23
LC record available at https://lccn.loc.gov/2016053678

ISBN 978-1-5072-0327-9
ISBN 978-1-5072-0328-6 (ebook)

To Rex Stout (1886–1975),
for reasons which must appear obvious;
and to Louise A. Estleman (1918–2002),
with eternal thanks; this time,
for awakening me to the world of the mystery.

"You are simply too conceited, too eccentric,
and too fat to work for!"

—ARCHIE GOODWIN

"Pfui!"

—NERO WOLFE

A LEGACY:
AND HOW TO TWIST IT (ALMOST)
BEYOND RECOGNITION

Preface by Loren D. Estleman

Back in 1992, an editor at Bantam Books asked me to take part in a reissue of Rex Stout's Nero Wolfe mysteries with introductions written by other writers in the field, appended to their novels of choice. I jumped at the chance, both because I was in excellent company and because I've been a Wolfe buff ever since my mother subscribed to *Ellery Queen's Mystery Magazine* when I was a boy. A good month was one that brought a new Wolfe novella into that 1867 farmhouse. The mash-up of old-school cerebral bloodhound (Wolfe) and American-style hardboiled dick (Archie Goodwin) addressed my interest in both forms.

I was given my choice of which book to introduce, so I selected *Fer-de-Lance*, the first in the series. On the one hand, I was busy at the time, and since I'd reread that one recently, I wouldn't be required to do extra homework. On the other, more important hand (my right, if it matters; it would to Wolfe), weighing in on the first appearance of Wolfe and Archie Goodwin, his loyal operative, secretary, and all-around dogsbody, gave me the opportunity to comment on life in general in the brownstone on West Thirty-Fifth

Street where for forty years the master of the house tended to his orchids, drank beer, ate (and sometimes prepared) elegant meals three times a day, and nabbed the occasional murderer; where his snarky assistant kept the germination records, mother-henned the bank account, did the legwork, and provided muscle when it was required; where Theodore Horstmann oversaw the floral display on the roof twenty-four hours a day, as opposed to Wolfe's four; and where Fritz Brenner, a chef who could have written his ticket in any five-star restaurant in the world, bickered with the boss about how to roast songbirds [!] and opened the front door to admit (and sometimes refuse admittance to) clients, cops, doctors, lawyers, and murderers.

As I said in that introduction—which because of the book's reptilian angle and the then-current popularity of a TV melodrama I wanted to call "Snakes and the Fat Man," but was overruled—there's something particularly cozy about that agoraphobic setup, where the routine never changed from 1934 to 1976, and where no one aged. A quarter of a century ago, I saw the advantage, as did Archie, of remaining thirty-three forever.

The life may have been a little *too* cozy. In *And Be a Villain*, Goodwin arises moderately early for a stakeout, skips breakfast, and by seven fifteen A.M. is nearly prostrate with hunger. The scene reminded me of one in the Sax Rohmer Fu Manchu series, in which an observer marvels that a man kept in suspended animation for three days hadn't succumbed to starvation. A woman and daughter sharing the scene in *Villain* are presented in the same predicament. Stout must have been a great proponent of the "most important meal of the day"; I'm content with coffee and orange juice.

That introduction, by the way, cost me $400.

I was paid $200 to write it, and while laying the groundwork began to obsess about that massive globe in Wolfe's office, and the knowledge that one like it was available in my favorite rare bookstore, priced at $600. I bought it, and don't regret it; the thing lights up, casting a warm yellow glow over my study in the evening and fueling my fantasies of being invited to join Wolfe and Archie on one of their adventures; the first's cerebral, the second's as action-filled as a Bruce Willis film. (Well, almost; I can picture Archie scorning an umpteenth gallop down flights of fire stairs and absenting himself to report to the boss.)

Some critics have taken Stout to task for foisting tepid, easily guessed perpetrators on his readers, depending overmuch on the vividness of his recurring cast to hold his audience. This may be true; although career mystery writer that I am, I'm frequently at a loss to solve mysteries written by colleagues.

Robert B. Parker, in his own introduction to one of the reprints, made the telling point that while the regulars are sharply defined, the gaggle of temporary guests who convene in Wolfe's office for the final reveal are often interchangeable and difficult to separate from one another; and with this I agree. It may have something to do with the choice of names: Sorting the Jasper Pines from the Nathan Traubs and the Deborah Koppels from the Helen Grants is challenging, either by similarity of cadence or the faint suspicion that their creator didn't put much time into the christening.

I don't care, somehow; and somehow, it seems, neither does anyone else. Sherlock Holmes built up his following not so much from his cases and their *dramatis personae* as from the cozy clutter of the sitting room at 221B, Baker Street, and the fog-choked medieval streets of Victorian London. Many of us are more interested in what exotic concoction Fritz is laying out on the dinner table than in who slew Auntie Roo.

❧

Which explains why the Wolfe novellas tend to leave me cold. The foreshortening demands a greater emphasis on plot and a lesser one on character. The plush surroundings of Wolfe's office, the intriguing layout of the Manhattan brownstone that constituted his world, and the repartee between master detective and capable assistant and squabbles between homeowner and cook are sketchy at best. I love short fiction, but a man of Wolfe's girth needs room to swing his elbows.

In any case I find the novella form half-developed at best, like an egg that Wolfe would judge under-poached. With a bit of encouragement, it could aspire to become a novel. With ruthless editing, it could stand as a meaty short story. As it stands, it manages to be both flabby and gaunt.

Wolfe and Goodwin's thorny relationship—there is no worshipful Dr. Watson here—provides many of the series' comic moments, and underscores its verisimilitude: After all, who has *not* worked for a boss who needed a dressing-down from time to time, had the employee the grit to do it? In another genre where I dabble, I patterned the scenes between Page Murdock, deputy U.S. marshal, and his brilliant and egotistical superior, Judge Harlan A. Blackthorne of Montana Territory, on these exchanges. Theirs, too, is a partnership made up of equal parts exasperation and respect.

I'm not sure if the Bantam assignment is when the ghost of the germ of the concept that became Claudius Lyon first materialized; but all the necessary materials were certainly in place, like the various nutrients and whatnot required to grow orchids.

Similar ground had already been broken. Sir Arthur Conan Doyle's greatest creation may not have been the first popular character to inspire tributes and parodies, but he must be the most prolific. Disregarding the many affectionate send-ups that appeared while Holmes was still sleuthing, I'll direct the reader's attention to August Derleth's deferential Solar Pons mysteries and Robert L. Fish's infuriatingly hilarious Schlock Homes burlesques, dripping with inside puns (*The Sound of the Basketballs* is my favorite) laced with vaudevillian Yiddish. Stout himself entered the fold with numerous sly hints that Wolfe was the illegitimate offspring of Holmes and old flame Irene Adler during the former's Asian hiatus following his supposed death at the Reichenbach Falls.

Nor was I the first to consider abducting Wolfe and Goodwin for my own nefarious purposes. John Lescroart's *Son of Holmes*, featuring a Wolfian household sired by Sherlock's sluggish obese brother Mycroft, and Robert Goldsborough's extension of the Wolfe series by commission of the Stout estate—a brief experiment in the dubious tradition of sucking all the remaining blood out of a distinguished career—come to mind.

These were straight-faced pastiches, intended to pay *hommage* to the originals. To my knowledge, no one yet had attempted the Fish approach, giving thanks for the buggy ride by way of poking affectionate fun at the driver. Mind you, I had some reservations, when "Who's Afraid of Nero Wolfe" was published in the June 2008 issue of *Ellery Queen's Mystery Magazine*, that by the close of summer I'd be chased into the mountains by humorless Wolfe aficionados bearing torches and pitchforks; but when the Wolfe Pack, a national organization founded to honor Stout's best-known work, invited me to attend its annual convention in New York City (I declined with deep reluctance, being previously engaged), and assured I mustn't expect a necktie party in my honor—quite the opposite—I sighed in relief.

I shouldn't have worried. Anyone who'd stick with the series long enough to form an attachment must share Archie Goodwin's acerbic sense of humor, knowing how much it abraded his employer's image of himself as the Albert Einstein of detection. Such a loyalist would forgive, perhaps even embrace, the tableau of hero-worshipping nebbish Claudius Lyon, shady leech Arnie Woodbine, and kosher chef Gus, sharing a Brooklyn townhouse with the tomato plants flourishing on the roof despite Lyon's botanical ineptitude.

Right away I jettisoned homicide from the template, both to keep it light and because word problems and logistical conundrums seemed more suitable to a puzzle fan pretending to be a world-class detective. In place of the danger inherent in attempting to outsmart a murderer, I ramped up the threat factor represented by Inspector Cramer in the Wolfes, fashioning Captain Stoddard of the Brooklyn Bunco Squad into a vindictive bully determined to catch Lyon and Woodbine in the act of accepting payment for investigative services rendered without a license. Hardly the impervious rock of the Stout series, Lyon's mortal dread of thuggish authority figures, and Woodbine's criminal record, disinclines him to pursue Goodwin's favorite hobby of goading the local fuzz. Most of us can identify and sympathize with a character who has a healthy fear of men with badges and guns.

Whether our fitness-challenged hero is nuts or merely an admirer emulating *his* hero is open to question. Woodbine inclines toward the former, but if that's the case his affliction hasn't restricted his ability to reason. Despite his absurdity, he's the smartest man in any room—as long as that room doesn't contain Wolfe. He'd be pretty hard to take if he just kept blundering, Three Stooges fashion, into success in spite of himself. I hope readers agree when I say that when he pulls off a coup, astonishing his detractors, we feel as proud as if he were our own awkward child.

Who can question his motives? What's wrong with maintaining the same comfortable schedule five days a week, dining like a prince three times a day, puttering in a sunlit room mornings and afternoons, and exercising one's cognitive abilities solving the occasional mystery, especially when one has an Archie/Arnie to dispatch to face the hazards inherent? Such a life must be almost as enjoyable to lead as to write about.

"Wolfe Whistle," the tenth story following this preface, was written especially for this collection. It appears here for the first time. It may be the last to feature Lyon, as I'm running out of punny titles based on the word *wolf.* (Without exception, they have provided springboards to the plots.) I welcome suggestions, and if any appeals, I will give due credit to the source, unless the muse in question should prefer to remain anonymous.

Perhaps I sell myself short. Rex Stout seemed never at a loss for the tag most appropriate to the problem at hand. (My all-time favorite? *Trio for Blunt Instruments.*) But as long as I get to play make-believe, like Claudius Lyon, and walk in the footsteps of the master, maybe I'll keep finding them.

WHO'S AFRAID OF NERO WOLFE?

"Are you familiar with the work of a writer named Rex Stout?"

There were a hundred good reasons not to answer the Help Wanted notice in the *Habitual Handicapper*, and only one to answer it; but answer it I did, because I'd been canned for gambling on company time and I was on parole.

The text was brief:

Nimble-witted man needed for multitudinous duties.
Salary commensurate with skill. Room and meals
included. Apply at 700 Avenue J, Flatbush.

Seven hundred was a townhouse, one of those anonymous sandstone jobs standing in a row like widows at a singles club. It ran to three stories and a half-submerged basement, with glass partitions on the roof for a garden or something. A balding party in a cutaway coat someone had forgotten to return to the rental place answered the doorbell. "Who are you, I should ask?"

I took a header on the accent and replied in Yiddish. "Arnie Woodbine, nimble of wit." I held up the sheet folded to the advertisement.

"Mr. Lyon is in the plant rooms ten minutes more," he said, in Yiddish also. "In the office you can wait."

I followed him down a hall and through the door he opened, into a big room furnished as both office and parlor, with a big desk that looked as if it had been carved out of a solid slab of mahogany, rows of oak file cabinets, scattered armchairs, a big green sofa, and a huge globe in a cradle in one corner, plastered all over with countries that hadn't existed since they gassed all the pet rocks.

As I sat, in an orange leather chair that barely let my feet touch the floor, I came down with a dose of déjà vu. There was something familiar about the setup, but it was as tough to pin down as a dream. Whatever it was it put my freakometer in the red zone. I was set to fly the coop when something started humming, the walls shook, a paneled section slid open, and I got my first look at Claudius Lyon.

He was the best-tailored beach ball I'd ever met: five feet from top to bottom and from side to side in a mauve three-piece with a green silk necktie and pocket square, soft cordovans on his tiny feet. His face was as round as a baby's, with no more sign of everyday wear-and-tear than a baby's had. He was carrying something in a clay pot. I was pretty sure it was a tomato plant.

On his way from the elevator he reached up without pausing to straighten a picture that had been knocked crooked by the vibration in the shaft. So far I didn't exist, but when he finished arranging the pot on the corner of his desk and with a little hop mounted the nearest thing I'd ever seen to a La-Z-Boy on a swivel, he fixed me with bright eyes and introduced himself. He didn't offer to shake hands.

When I told him my name, he grinned from ear to ear, a considerable expanse. "Indeed," he squeaked.

I didn't know why at the time, but I was dead sure I already had the job.

He asked about my work experience. I gave him an honest answer. I'm always honest about my dishonesty when I'm not actually practicing it. "I'm a good confidence man in the second class and a first-class forger. I've got diplomas from two institutions to prove it. I don't have them on me, but you can confirm it by calling my parole officer."

He dug a finger inside his left ear, a gesture I would get to know as a sign his brain was in overdrive. The faster and more industriously he dug, the more energy his gray cells were putting out.

When he finished he offered me refreshment. "This is the time of day for my first cream soda."

I declined, not adding that there's no time of day when I'd ever consent to join him in one, or anyone else. He startled me then by turning his head and shouting, "Gus!" I'd assumed he'd tug on a bell rope or something. The balding gent in the rusty tailcoat entered a minute later carrying a tray with a can on it and a Bamm-Bamm glass. He took the tray away empty and Lyon poured, drank, and belched discreetly into his green pocket square. He folded and tucked it back in place.

"I admire candor, up to a point." With a show of fastidiousness, he twisted the pop-top loose from the can, placed it inside his desk drawer, and pushed the drawer shut with his belly. "Yours falls just to the left of that. As it happens, a man who can sell another man a bill of goods would be valuable to this agency. I can also foresee a time when an aptitude with a pen would toe the mark."

"What agency's that?"

He lifted the place where eyebrows belonged. "Why, a detective agency, of course. What did you think the job was?"

The coin dropped into the pan; I knew what it was about the situation at 700 Avenue J, from the layout to the funny business with the pop-top, that sent centipedes marching up my spine. Claudius Lyon clinched it with his next question.

"Are you familiar with the work of a writer named Rex Stout?"

⚜

That was three years ago. My debt to the State of New York is square, so thank God I don't have to keep convincing my PO that my association with a screwball like Lyon is legit.

The sticking point was my felon status, and the impossibility of ever qualifying for a license as a private investigator. Lyon hasn't one, either, lacking as he does the professional experience. He gets around it by not charging for his services.

It's no hardship, because he's as rich as the dame who writes the Harry Potter books. His old man had made certain improvements to the gasket that sealed the Cass-O-Matic pressure cooker, which is no longer in manufacture, but NASA has adapted the improvements to the space shuttle, and since the inventor is also no longer in circulation, the royalties come in to Lyon regular as the water bill.

I know what I'm talking about, because it's my job to deposit the checks in his account. I ordered a DEPOSIT ONLY stamp and charged it to household expenses, but I never use it. Lyon's signature is childlike, absurdly easy to duplicate on the endorsement, and I round the amount deposited to the nearest thousand and pocket the difference. It can be as little as a few bucks or as much as a couple of hundred, and if we ever decide to go our separate ways I can afford to coast for a year or so before I have to turn again to the Help Wanted section.

Claudius Lyon is obsessed with the writings of Rex Stout, or more particularly those of Archie Goodwin, who Stout represented as literary agent until Stout's death. Goodwin recorded the cases he'd helped solve for his employer, Nero Wolfe, a fat lethargic genius who grows orchids on the roof of his New York City brownstone, drinks beer by the bucket, eats tons of gourmet food prepared by Fritz, his Swiss chef and major-domo, and makes expenses by unraveling complex mysteries put to him by desperate clients, many of them well-heeled. Wolfe rarely leaves home and pays Goodwin to perform as his legman and general factotum.

To a fat little boy growing up in Brooklyn, Nero Wolfe was the nuts. Lyon loved to read mysteries, but he knew he'd never have the energy to emulate Sherlock Holmes, or the physique to withstand and deliver beatings a la Sam Spade and Philip Marlowe, or the good looks to seduce pertinent information out of swoony female suspects like the Saint. Wolfe's obesity and sedentary habits, however, suited Lyon right down to his wide bottom.

Some weeks before we met, Lyon had bought the townhouse, had it retrofitted to resemble Wolfe's sanctum, and changed his name legally to echo his hero's; Claudius, like Nero, was a lesser Roman emperor, and he felt he'd improved on the original by choosing a surname inspired by a predator more closely associated with the circuses of Rome. I haven't asked him what name he'd gone by before that. The bureaucrat who sends his checks had been wised up, he himself hasn't seen fit to volunteer anything, and while I firmly believe that the contents of another man's wallet might as well be mine, the secrets of his past are his own. To quote Lyon: "Discretion and integrity are not solely the province of the law-abiding."

I might not be working for him if Arnie Woodbine and Archie Goodwin didn't look like the same name if you squinted at it and took your eyes out of focus. He was especially pleased to learn that it's Arnie, not Arnold, on my birth certificate; Goodwin had not been born Archibald.

But maybe I doubt too much. The notice I'd read in the racing sheet had appeared for a week in *The New York Times*, *Daily News*, and the Brooklyn rags, and had bought only disappointment in the form of an army of errand boys whose wits were about as nimble as a lawn-roller, and one feminist who protested Lyon's insistence on hiring a man. (Gus told me the master of the house hid in the plant room until she was ejected.) I'm shorter than Goodwin, not in as good shape, and have a cauliflower ear courtesy of an early disgruntled mark that makes it more of a challenge for me to charm women; but at least I'm not a feminist, and my wit has been known to turn a respectable cartwheel from time to time.

I'm one of his lesser compromises. To begin with, he has no tolerance for adult beverages. Even the so-called nonalcoholic beers blur his judgment, and one bottle of Wolfe's brand of choice might send him skipping naked through Coney Island singing "Wind Beneath My Wings." He drinks the cream soda that's contributed in no small part to his lard, and keeps track of his consumption by counting the pop-tops in his desk, just as Wolfe does his bottle caps.

His other substitutions are strictly personal prejudice:

1. Wolfe's favorite color is yellow; Lyon prefers green, and overdoes it. With all the red in the rare old office rug hand-woven by the Mandan tribe—which was wiped out by smallpox two minutes

after the first European sneezed on it, hence the rarity—all those strong shades of green dotted about look like Christmas year-round;

2. Gus is no Fritz in the kitchen, although his repertoire of kosher recipes is prodigious;

3. The heartiest strain of orchid withers and turns black when it sees Lyon coming. Roses aren't much less difficult. By the time I came along he'd begun cultivating tomatoes, which Gus tries his best to make work with gefilte fish.

Lyon's brown thumb has spared him the ordeal of replicating Theodore Horstmann, Wolfe's resident expert on orchids. Tomatoes require no maintenance beyond watering, fertilizing, and spraying for bugs, and he spends most of his two hours in the morning and two hours in the afternoon on the roof watching *Martin Kane, Private Eye* on video. I've taken dozens of letters at his dictation urging all the networks to revive the series.

So with my introduction into the household, the metamorphosis was complete, if skewed a bit. You'd think he'd have been as happy as a Wisconsin nut in a Waldorf salad. Instead he went into a tailspin that took all the manic out of his depression for weeks, and with sound reason—or anyone as sound as his reason ever got.

No mystery.

He'd placed another advertisement in all the regulars and the *Habitual Handicapper:*

Vexed? Stymied? Up a tree? Consult Claudius Lyon,
the world's greatest amateur detective. No fees
charged. Your satisfaction is my reward. Apply in
person at 700 Avenue J, Flatbush.

The notice ran for weeks, during which time Jimmy Hoffa could have camped out on the stoop with no risk of discovery by a visitor. At Lyon's prodding I made several trips outside to push the doorbell to make sure it was working. It rang with a kind of *ha-ha* the little fatty couldn't have appreciated very much.

"Try taking out the 'amateur,'" I suggested. "People think if you don't charge anything, that's all your services are worth."

"I'm unlicensed."

"I didn't say send them a bill. Just don't say you don't in the ad."

"The phrase 'the world's greatest detective' would violate the truth-in-advertising laws. Nero Wolfe is still practicing, and he is demonstrably the world's finest in his profession."

"Who's afraid of Nero Wolfe?" I sang.

"I am. When he learns I've counterfeited his life and livelihood, I fully expect a visit from Nathaniel Parker, his attorney. Since I do not claim to *be* Nero Wolfe, I cannot be accused of theft of identity, and because I accept no emolument for my efforts on behalf of my clients, I am not guilty of fraud. So long as I stay within the law, I'm a fleabite on Wolfe's thick hide, nothing more. To stray over the line would bring doom upon this roof." He slumped in his oversize chair, looking like Humpty Dumpty at the base of the wall.

I let him sulk, opened the laptop on my desk, and pecked out this gem:

Mystified? Claudius Lyon never is. See for yourself.
No fees charged where satisfaction is not met. Apply,
etc.

I showed him the printout. I hadn't seen him smile like that since I'd told him my name. Remember, I'm a first-class second-class con man; although I had to strangle my basic instincts to dupe people into thinking it might cost them when it wouldn't. It's a

Bizarro World, that billet. I e-mailed the text to all the sheets, then opened the dictionary program Lyon had installed and decided *emolument* is a good word.

That was Thursday. On Friday we had our first client.

❧

Raymond Nurls's percentage of body fat wouldn't have fried a lox in Gus's skillet. In his three-button black suit he made a dividing line in the center of the guest chair, which was another of those areas where Lyon's attempt to clone Nero Wolfe's life had gone south. He'd hired a colorblind upholsterer, who covered it in orange. It clashed with the scarlet in the Mandan rug like our two cultures.

Nurls was halfway through his twenties but well on his way toward crabby old age, with hair mowed to the edge of baldness and a silver chain clipped to the legs of his glasses. He steepled his hands when he spoke.

"I assumed from your advertisement you're either a detective or a magician. Which is it?"

Lyon tried to lower his lids, but he was too jazzed by the prospect of work to keep them from flapping back up like cheap window shades. "I don't pull rabbits out of hats, but I can tell you how it's done."

I leaned out from my word processor, where I was taking notes. "That means he's a detective."

"Very good. I'm the executive director of the American Poetical Association. Perhaps you've heard of it."

But unless it advertised in his complete run of Doubleday Crime Club editions, Lyon hadn't, so Nurls filled us in. The APA was an organization devoted to art patronage, specifically for poets who'd missed the memo that the road to starvation begins with the purchase of one's first rhyming dictionary. Its purpose was to mooch money from people who'd run out of places to store it and provide grants to support promising talent until their work was ready for publication. To me it seemed cruel to jolly them along only to cut them loose just when their unsold copies were on the way back to the pulp mill, but then my mind wandered after the part about separating the rich from their wealth, so I may have missed some of the fine points. I dislike competition.

Once a year, the association threw a dinner in a hotel in Canarsie, where the winner of the coveted Van Dusen Prize for Outstanding Poetry received a plaque and a check for $10,000. I imagine that mollified some landlord. Certainly it reawakened my interest.

At this point Lyon swooped in for the kill. "Which was stolen, the plaque or the check?"

"Neither."

Lyon yelled for cream soda.

"I'm new to the Association," said Nurls, when Gus left with his empty tray. "I replaced the executive director who'd been with the APA since the beginning, who retired rather suddenly to Arizona on the advice of his cardiologist. My first duty is to plan this year's dinner, which will commemorate the twenty-fifth anniversary of our founding. Naturally I spent a great deal of time on the phone with my predecessor, gathering historical details to include in the program: names of charter members, events of note, etc. Naturally a complete list of past winners of the Van Dusen Prize was essential."

"Naturally," Lyon and I said simultaneously. He scowled at me and I returned my attention to my screen.

Walter Van Dusen, we learned, was a loaded industrialist jonesing for culture, who upon his death had left an endowment that made the cash incentive possible. Before that, the winners had taken home a plaque only, presumably to boil the sap from to make soup.

"When I came aboard," Nurls went on, "the records situation was rustic, to put it charitably. The old fellow had taken them with him, for reasons of his own; I picture a shabby notebook in his personal shorthand. I rang him up in Phoenix, and he read off the winners' names and contact information where it existed. I thought it would be a grand gesture to invite as many of them as were available to attend the dinner as guests of the Association."

He related the tragic circumstances: Of twenty-four former winning poets, eleven could not be located, six had died from natural causes, three had committed suicide, and two weren't interested; one, over the phone, had been emphatic on the subject to the point of questioning the details of Raymond Nurls's ancestry. Of the pair remaining, one was too elderly to make the trip. The last was willing, but required mileage and accommodations. These the executive director agreed to provide, since the budget was flush.

"I'm concerned chiefly with one of the names on the list," Nurls said. "A gentleman named Noah Ward."

"Dead, disgruntled, or unlocatable?" Lyon asked.

"The last. So far, I've been unable to learn anything about him. I Googled the name, and was able to narrow the list to three who have any connection with literary endeavor, but one is far too young—he'd have been in junior high the year Ward was honored, and our prize committee is not disposed to recognize precociousness—another, the editor of the book review page of a Baltimore literary journal, assured me he'd never written poetry and didn't review it because, quote, 'I wouldn't know a grand epic from subway doggerel,' unquote. The third, a self-published suspense writer, thought the APA had something to do with the Humane Society." He adjusted his glasses.

Lyon shifted his weight, evidently in sympathetic discomfort with this last piece of intelligence. Actually he was trying to burst a bubble in his gut, which he did, with spectacular results. In a belching contest I'd put every cent I've embezzled from him on his nose. "Why this obsession with one name on the list?"

"Because Ward is the only one on it I've been unable to confirm ever existed."

"Ah."

Encouraged, the executive director steepled his hands higher. "Nary a birth certificate nor a social security number nor a school transcript nor an arrest record nor so much as a ticket for overtime parking. Really, Mr. Lyons—"

"Lyon. I am singular, not plural."

"I stand corrected. It's next to impossible, not to say impossible, to exist in today's world without leaving a footprint of some kind on the Internet. Therefore I propose that Noah Ward is a chimera."

"And this is significant because—?"

"You're a detective. Figure it out. Whoever claimed that ten-thousand-dollar prize under a fictitious name is guilty of grand fraud."

"I assume you've ruled out the likelihood of a pseudonym."

"At once. The rules of the American Poetical Association expressly state that all work must be submitted under the contestant's legal name. The provision was adopted to prevent anyone from submitting more than one work for consideration. A long lead time was established between the deadline for entry and the announcement of the winner to investigate the identities of all the contributors."

"Your predecessor could not enlighten you on the details?"

Nurls jammed his glasses farther into his head. "He perished last week, in a fire that consumed his condominium, himself, and any records that might have furnished additional information. The disaster was entirely accidental," he added, when Lyon's eyes brightened. "The arson investigators traced it to a faulty electrical circuit."

His host pouted. "Unfortunate and tragic. I assume you polled the membership for reminiscences? The committee responsible for the honor springs to mind."

"Our membership rolls run toward an older demographic. Everyone who might have shed light upon the selection has passed. The only member I managed to reach who was present at that dinner is unreliable." He touched his left temple.

"Dear me. All the powers appear to be aligned against you. Is it your intention to bring legal action for the recovery of the ten thousand?"

"It is. The Association has empowered me, upon filing formal charges, to remit fifteen percent to the party who identifies and exposes the guilty person. Expenses added, of course." Nurls sat back a tenth of an inch, folding his hands on his spare middle.

Lyon finished his cream soda in one long draft, this time patted back the burp, and replaced his pocket square with all the ceremony of a color guard folding the flag. "I accept the challenge, Mr. Nurls. We'll discuss payment upon success or an admission of failure. In the latter event I will accept no remuneration."

I had to hand it to the little balloon. He'd managed to appear professional and hold off the wrath of the State of New York in one elegant speech. I knew him then for a liar when he said he couldn't pull a rabbit out of a hat. But the bean counter in the ugly orange chair wouldn't have taken the Holy Annunciation at face value if Gabriel had blown sixteen bars in his ear. He'd have asked for references, and followed up on them on Yahoo!

"How do I know you can deliver? Forgive me, but all I have to go on is three lines in the *Times*."

Lyon looked at the clock. "It's nearly lunchtime. Chicken soup, with a stock combined of livers and gizzards; free-range poultry, of course. Cheese blintzes for dessert and an acceptable Manischewitz from my cellar. Once you've sampled the fare of my table, you'll be in a better position to judge my success in this profession. Will you join us?"

Nurls declined, looking a shade green around the collar; but he was hooked. Me, too, from then on. A first-rate, second-rate grifter knows a champ when he sees one.

❧

"Phooey!"

Wolfe says, "Pfui," but his disciple can't pronounce the labial without spraying.

He was responding to my suggestion to access the Library of Congress website for poetical compositions copyrighted under the name Noah Ward.

"It's futile to attempt to prove a man does not exist. It expends energy the way trying to add light to dark wastes paint, with no appreciable effect. We'll assume as a hypothesis that Nurls is right and Ward is a phantasm."

"How'd you know that about paint?" I asked.

"I investigated the phenomenon of temporary employment the summer I turned fifteen. A less than august August." He dismissed the subject with a wave of his little finger. "If a check was issued to Noah Ward, someone had to cash it. The transaction took place too far in the past for any bank to retain a record of it, even if we found the bank and its personnel were willing to cooperate. March down to the police station and inquire whether anyone using that name or something similar has ever been arrested for bunco steering."

"These days they just call it fraud."

"Indeed? Colorless. A pity."

"Ever's a long way to comb back, even if I could get them to do it."

"Concentrate on the past seven years. I assume that's still the statute of limitations for most crimes. A man who draws water once may be expected to return to the well the next time he thirsts. Perhaps he wasn't so successful the second time."

"What if the well isn't in Brooklyn?"

"Start here. Unless and until he has the money in hand, a poet is unlikely to come by the travel expenses necessary to collect. My *Ode on a* Lycopersicon esculentum paid only in copies of the *Herbivoron*."

Before taking my leave I looked up all three unfamiliar words, identifying the Latin preferred name of the common tomato and the semimonthly newsletter issued by the Garden Fruit Council of New Jersey.

I have cop friends. I've been down there often enough to strike up acquaintances and I have a good line of gab, which they like almost as much as Krispy Kreme and are apt to disregard a little thing like a nonviolent rap sheet in order to enjoy it. I cast my line and caught a big fish, although I didn't know it at the time and would have thrown it back if I had.

❧

It was Friday night. For religious reasons Gus couldn't clock in again until after sundown Saturday, and unlike his hero, Lyon is capable of burning a salad, so I fixed him two boxes of mac and cheese in the microwave and made myself a BLT. I can keep kosher as well as the next guy, but every so often I get a craving for swine and shellfish that has to be addressed.

We were just finishing up when the doorbell rang. It rang again before we remembered Gus couldn't answer it. By the time I got to the door our visitor had abandoned ringing for banging. I used the peephole and hustled back to the dining room.

"It's cops," I said. "Actually only one, but what he lacks in number he makes up for in mean."

Lyon glared up at me from his tilted bowl. I shook my head innocently. I hadn't tried to sell anyone an autographed *Portable Chaucer* in six months.

I brought Captain Stoddard into the office, where Lyon was just clambering onto his perch behind the desk. I was halfway through introductions when our visitor brought his fist down on the leather top. "Where do you get off sending this cheap crook to my precinct? I put every officer who gave him the time of day on report."

"Please have a seat, sir. I have spinal issues that make it agony to tilt my head back more than three degrees." His tone wobbled a little. He seemed to have authority issues as well, but I gave him points for the show of spunk.

Stoddard did, too, maybe, or maybe he'd been on report himself too many times that fiscal period for pushing around citizens. Anyway, he sat.

Physically, he's the opposite of Nero Wolfe's nemesis in NYPD Homicide. Inspector Cramer is beefy where Captain Stoddard is gaunt, and the captain's a few more years away from mandatory retirement, but he filled the orange chair with nastiness the way Cramer fills the famous red one with buttock. Stoddard commands the local precinct. I was trying out the straight-and-narrow as much to avoid another interrogation by him as to stay out of jail.

"Woodbine left your name," he told Lyon. "So far I can't find a record under it, but if you're partnered up with this little goldbrick artist I'll start one for you personally. What kind of scam you got going that involves turning the Brooklyn Police Department into an information service?"

"I pay taxes, Mr. Stoddard. If you look up my name outside your rogues' gallery, you may be able to calculate how much. But even the poorest resident of this country has the right to consult the police when he suspects a law has been broken."

He gulped, but he got it out. It was a good speech, too. The proof was in the way the man he spoke it to didn't haul him out of his chair and slam-dunk him into his own recycling bin. Instead his nails dug little semicircles in the pumpkin-colored leather.

"I monitor all the computers in the precinct," he growled. "Some cops think that when I step out they can fool around in the files and get away with it. They always fold when I jump them. Who's this bird Ward?"

Spunk has its limits. Lyon looked to me for support, but I was scareder than he was, with experience to justify it. He took a couple of deep breaths to prevent hyperventilating and told Stoddard everything Raymond Nurls had told us. He'd barely finished when the captain sprang to his feet with an Anglo-Saxon outburst that knocked out of line the picture on the wall next to the elevator shaft. I'd thought only the elevator could do that.

"A puzzle!" he roared. "My precinct has murders to investigate, rapes, child abuse, armed robbery, each of which requires three weeks minimum to make an arrest and a case to make it stick, not counting petty little interruptions like burglary, purse-snatching, and assault, and you take up twenty minutes of that time playing Scrabble."

"You're being metaphorical, of course," Lyon put in. "Fraud is not a parlor game."

The fist came down, jumping a pen out of its little onyx skull. Lyon jumped too and looked ill. "A cheesy award given out by a bunch of nancies for the best poim about a lark. No!" Fist. The pen rolled to the edge of Lyon's blotter.

The little butterball surprised me. Ever since Stoddard had leapt up he'd been doing his best to shrink himself inside his folds of suet, like an armadillo gathering itself into a ball. Now his eyes opened wide and he straightened himself in his chair, tilting his head back two degrees past agony to meet the glare of his tormentor. "Would you repeat what you just said?"

Stoddard wound back the tape a little too far, back to the unbroadcastable word that had brought him out of his chair.

"After that," Lyon said. His tone was as steady as the tide. "After I questioned your choice of the word Scrabble."

"An award! A cheesy award!" The captain shouted into his face, flecks of spittle spattering him from his hairline to the knot of his green silk tie. "Are you deaf, too? I *know* you're dumb!"

"Thank you, Mr. Stoddard. You are a synaptic savant."

That silenced him. It silenced me, too, until I looked up both words on the dictionary program. He straightened, looking around.

"Where's your investigator's license? You're supposed to display it prominently."

"I haven't one."

Stoddard's bony face twisted to make room for a horse-toothed grin. It wasn't nice. He isn't a nice man, or even a good one. He lowered his tone to conversational level; he might have been bidding four, no trump. "Do you know the penalty in this state for conducting professional investigations without a license?"

"I've never had cause to look it up. A professional would be well advised to do so, but I don't charge for my services. My amateur standing remains intact."

The horse teeth receded. Stoddard's BB eyes darted left, then right. That put me inside range. "What about Woodbine? Don't tell me he works for you for free. He'd walk to Albany and back for a dirty dollar."

"I employ Mr. Woodbine to obtain the information I require to pursue my avocation."

"That's investigation. You need a license to earn a salary."

"Tish-tush." I gave Lyon double points for that; thumbing his nose to the NYPD while employing a phrase alien to his inspiration. At his insistence I'd made a sizeable dent in his Rex Stout library, and had not once come across it. Somewhere in that roly-poly wad of derivative flapdoodle was an authentic original waiting to be recognized, as well as a tough little nut. "When a personal assistant is asked to pick up the telephone and inquire when a bank closes, is he conducting an illegal investigation or running an errand? Is it your desire to give up your day off to answer that question at a public hearing?"

I never found out if Stoddard had an answer for that. He opened his mouth, presumably to let out a four-letter opinion of the question that had been put to him, but he closed it. Lyon's eyes were shut tight, and he was foraging inside his left ear with the energy of an anteater.

⚜

Nero Wolfe never sums up a case without an audience. It can contain a handful or a horde, but it rarely gathers outside his personal throne room, where the Great Detective holds forth from behind the massive desk on West Thirty-Fifth Street, New York, New York. Claudius Lyon would have it no other way, even if the venue was his office of many compromises in Brooklyn, and his spectators reduced to four.

Stoddard was present, eager to make his case to prosecute Lyon and me for playing detective without saying Simon Says, as well as fraud, and of course Raymond Nurls was invited. My seat, turned from my desk, was a perk of the job, but I couldn't see any reason why Gus was there, except to fill one more seat in a show that needed a solid third act if it weren't to be left to die on the road. It had taken all of Lyon's powers of persuasion to convince the cook that he wouldn't burn in hell for sitting in on Shabbat. Just to make sure, Gus sat in the green chair nearest the door, where he could escape if anyone asked him to turn on a light or something. Nurls's thin frame bisected another green chair, and Stoddard deposited his 170 pounds of pure hostility in the orange.

Lyon entered last, straightened the picture on the wall, scowled at the pea-sized green tomato growing at the end of the vine in the pot on his desk, and scaled to his seat. "Thank you all for coming. Does anyone object to Mr. Woodbine taking notes?"

Nurls shook his head, the silver chain swaying on his glasses. Stoddard scooped a small portable cassette recorder out of his pocket and balanced it on his knee. "Just in case he misses something culpable," he said.

Lyon shrugged and cracked open the can I'd placed on the desk. He took a slug and began.

"Mr. Nurls. When was the Van Dusen Prize first presented?"

"Fifteen years ago this fall. It went to—"

"The American Poetical Association was then ten years old?"

"Yes. I don't see what this has to do with Noah Ward. He wasn't honored until years later."

"I will establish relevance presently. I suppose it goes without saying that before the existence of the ten-thousand-dollar honorarium, the encomium was not referred to as a prize."

"It does, and yet you said it. A prize without a prize is hardly a prize."

"Poetically put. How, then, was it referred to?"

"It was called the Golden Muse Award. The plaque still contains an etching in gold of Calliope and Erato, the—"

"Thank you. During our first conversation, you said the man you replaced as executive director had held that position since the APA was founded, is that correct?"

"Yes. Really, Mr. Lyon—"

This time Stoddard interrupted. "I'm with Poindexter. Connect this to a scam artist who conned the sissies out of a bundle."

"I beg your pardon, sir. That is not my intention."

Even Gus took his eyes off his escape route to stare at Lyon. Stoddard and Nurls started talking at once. I gave up trying to get it all down.

A pudgy palm came up for silence; the owner broke it himself when his voice squeaked. "I have been engaged to untangle the mystery that surrounds the elusive Noah Ward. I shall now proceed to do so. Mr. Nurls, when you spoke with your predecessor on the telephone, did he call the Van Dusen Prize by that name?"

Nurls started to speak, then adjusted his glasses and started again. "No. As a matter of fact he just called it 'the award.' I assume he did so out of habit."

"Not unusual for one long familiar with the original. How did he read off the names of past winners?"

"What do you mean?"

"Did he say, 'The Golden Muse Award in nineteen eighty-eight went to Joe Doakes,' 'The Golden Muse Award in nineteen eighty-nine went to Jane Doe,' and so on and so forth?"

"Certainly not. The conversation would have been interminable. He provided the year and the name in each instance, and I wrote them down."

Lyon drank, burped, wiped. "One of my abandoned interests is the history of the Pulitzer Prize for Literature. I gave up the study when it became clear that the board at Columbia University would never honor Rex Stout, or more appropriately Archie Goodwin for his many contributions to American letters. I do recall that in nineteen forty, when the director of the board objected to the others' choice of Ernest Hemingway's *For Whom the Bell Tolls*, it was decided that no prize would be issued that year. Are you aware if this ever happened in regard to the Van Dusen Prize or the Golden Muse?"

"It never did. The former executive director read off twenty-four years and twenty-four names. This year's winner has not yet been determined."

"I submit that it happened, and that he told you as much when he used the phrase you misunderstood for a man's name. The three syllables you interpreted as 'Noah Ward,' had they been spelled out, would in fact read—"

"No award." Nurls slumped in his seat. I hadn't thought his spine had that much play in it.

Stoddard shot to his feet. His tape recorder slid off his knee to the floor. "You took up my precinct's time and mine over a dumb-ass pun?"

"A homonym, to be precise. A hazard of oral communication."

"You and Woodbine are both under arrest for obstruction of justice."

Lyon's moon face was gray as cardboard, but he held his ground.

"Don't be absurd, Mr. Stoddard. I've prevented Mr. Nurls from obstructing justice unwittingly by filing a nuisance complaint. If there never was a Noah Ward, no fraud was perpetrated, and the APA simply reinvested the money that would have been awarded, assuring the continued existence of the Van Dusen Prize. I have you to thank for a signal accomplishment on my part."

"Don't drag me into it, you little blimp."

"No dragging is necessary, sir. Earlier today in this very room, you referred to the Van Dusen as an award, not a prize, and employed an emphatic 'No' to indicate your rejection of the importance of the affair to the police. You may have noticed that at that point I entered into a reverie."

"You stuck your finger in your ear."

"I find the action stimulates the cortex. Granted you hadn't a notion you were supplying a catalyst for the chemistry of my cognitive function, but that in no way diminishes your role in the outcome. I congratulate you."

"Bull. Since when is wordplay a signal accomplishment?"

"I must thank you again, for putting the question. In spite of the laws of physics, I have managed to change a tint of paint by adding a small amount of light to dark. In spite of Aristotle's philosophy, I have proven that someone never existed."

Nurls produced a checkbook, scribbled, and got up to place the check on Claudius Lyon's desk. "Two thousand, including a bonus for a job well done. You *are* a magician."

Captain Stoddard hovered. I wouldn't say he drooled, but he was ready to pounce the second Lyon touched the check.

The man behind the desk never looked at it. "Arnie, will you do the honors?"

I said I'd be pleased as punch. Nurls watched, astonished, Stoddard, boiling, as I tore the check sideways, lengthwise, and crosswise, and dropped the pieces into the wastebasket by my desk.

Stoddard slammed the door behind him, knocking crooked the picture on the wall. Lyon said goodbye to our client, rose, and straightened it on his way to the elevator.

THE BOY WHO CRIED WOLFE

"Get lost, Little Orphan Anything for a Buck."

The bomb dropped while I was card-indexing Claudius Lyon's latest contribution to horticultural science, a hybrid tomato plant that comprised all the disadvantages of a beefsteak and none of the advantages of a Roma, and Lyon, foundering up to his chins as usual behind his preposterously enormous desk, was pretending to read *The Portable Schopenhauer*. It was actually Carolyn Keene's *The Clue of the Dancing Puppet* inside the drab dust jacket, and he'd read it twice before in my tenure.

"Arnie," he said, "how long have you been working for me?"

I scowled at my new computer, a state-of-tomorrow's-art job that anticipates my mistakes and makes them for me. "Three years, two months, fifteen days, eleven minutes, and twenty-nine—no, thirty seconds."

"How much do you estimate you've embezzled from me during that period?"

The mouse skidded out from under my fingers.

He looked up from his book with his Gerber Baby smile. "I am a genius, but not an absent-minded one. I call my bank from time to time and occasionally balance my checkbook. When you deposit the royalties from NASA on my father's pressure-cooker gasket patent, you round down the amount and palm the rest. Absent a tedious study of the actual figures, I can arrive at a reasonable estimate by multiplying your time in my employ by the average sum pilfered. The product would support a modest harem."

"Well, it was a lark while it flew," I said finally. "Is it federal or local? I hear they put out a spread in the U.S. prisons. Anything beats Spam Saturday in Sing Sing."

"There's no need for bravado. I don't intend to pursue charges. With whom would I replace you? There is only one Arnie Woodbine, and Archie Goodwin is permanently off the market. I must make the best of my knockoff. Dock yourself ten dollars a week until the account is even."

"But that'll take—"

"Nine years, one month, twelve days, five hours, and thirty-two minutes. Consider it a long-term contract, which you'd be wise not to break." He returned to his reading.

In case anything about the foregoing seems familiar—not counting the larceny—now is a good time to point out that "Claudius Lyon" is an invention. The man who uses the name has remodeled his life to conform to that of his hero, Nero Wolfe of Manhattan, who raises orchids, employs a world-class chef, and solves mysteries brought to him by baffled clients. Lyon's own limitations have forced certain compromises: He grows tomatoes, eats kosher most of the time because that's all his chef, Gus, knows how to cook, and depends upon me, the poor man's Archie Goodwin (Wolfe's legman and hectoring angel), for mundane errands.

He's as fat as Wolfe but much shorter, and when he climbs into the big chair behind his desk he looks like Tweedledum with his legs swinging free. Not having any prior experience with geniuses, I don't know if he is one, but he's a damn clever little butterball who hasn't forgotten a thing he's learned from the thousands of whodunits he's read. I've seen him fall on his prat more than his share, but I've never seen him stumped.

Well, I had nothing better to do for the next nine years, one month, etc., and I'd been to prison and found it not up to my standards, so I didn't complain about the pay cut; instead I worked out an arrangement with Gus to buy generic lox and split the price difference. Lyon hasn't Wolfe's palate and wouldn't know the gourmet brand from Karl's Kut-Rate Kippers. It was a stingy little scam compared to the one I'd had going, even when I extended it to include gristly corned beef and day-old bagels, but it would do until something better came along. If you're the type who can live life on the level without gnawing your nails down to the knuckle, congratulations, and keep it to yourself. Without a dash of pepper the stew's just too flat.

The reason for all this chatter is it explains how the principal resident of the townhouse at 700 Avenue J, Flatbush, put his chubby little gray cells to work on the problem of William Thew.

❧

Gus's main motivator in our conspiracy was the convenience of not having to take the cross-town bus to the snooty little market that sold the best kosher in the five boroughs; the cheap stuff was available on the corner, and it delivered. I happened to answer the doorbell the day the pushy delivery boy showed up lugging a paper sack bigger than he was. I had to spread a bunch of celery to see his pinched little face under the obligatory backward baseball cap.

"Here, kid." I traded him a buck for the sack.

"My name's Jasper, not kid. Jasper Hull."

"The hell you say. You got that from an eighty-six-year-old man's obituary in the *Daily News*."

"It's Jasper just the same. I want to see Lyon."

"What's the matter, I don't tip big enough?"

"You call this a tip?" He pretended to blow his nose on George Washington, which even I thought was disrespectful; but I noticed he didn't throw it away. "I got a case for Lyon. He's a detective, ain't he? That's what it says in the Yellow Pages."

"It doesn't either. I wrote the ad. It says he provides answers to questions."

"If I got it that way, I'd've took my lousy buck and went. I seen all the fortunetellers I want to. They charge you up front and tell you a lot of bogus stuff that could mean anything."

"'Satisfaction guaranteed.' The ad says that too."

"Okay. Here." He held up the dollar.

"What's that for?"

"It's a what-do-you-call-it, a retainer."

I grinned. "Nice try, kid. Tell Captain Stoddard he's in violation of the child labor laws." I started to push the door shut, but damn if he didn't insert his wiry little body into the space. It was either squash him or stop. I considered the point and decided against squashing. It's hell on the finish.

I said, "You'd think the cops'd have enough to keep busy in a town like this without setting traps for one little fat guy with schizophrenic tendencies, but a month doesn't go by without the fuzz up top trying to trick Lyon into accepting payment and busting him for practicing private investigation without a license. Recruiting a kid's bad enough; a dollar's an insult to his intelligence. A fiver's plenty cute given the inflationary index. I'm surprised Stoddard didn't knock out a front tooth and give you a scruffy mutt from the pound."

"What's that mean?"

"It means get lost, Little Orphan Anything for a Buck." I leaned on the door. A little Mop & Glo can erase anything, even crushed adolescent.

He pushed back. Schlepping all that produce had made him strong as Gus's blood sausage. "How good can he be if he don't charge?"

"You're right. Now make like a tree and go away."

"I don't like cops neither," he said. "They say they're there to help, but all they do is write stuff down and shove it in a drawer. The detective agencies I tried won't listen to nobody but a grownup. I seen Lyon's name in the listing, and when this order came in where I work, I thought I'd take a shot."

"A shot at what?"

"Finding my father."

I had a comment about his father on the tip of my tongue, but I didn't spit it out. If I got Lyon a job right away worthy of his whacked-out brain, he might overlook a little chiseling on my part.

"Wipe your feet, kid." I opened the door wide.

❧

Lyon squeaked like a loose fan belt when I told him I'd parked a ten-year-old boy in the front room. To begin with he doesn't trust any creature his own size, and as for childhood he thinks it's a conspiracy to break valuable objects and make doorknobs sticky, which is a favorite phobia of his. He'd just come down from the plant room and hugged to his chest the specimen of the day in its fragile clay pot. "Get rid of him and spray Lysol on anything he might have touched. Children are the main carriers of most of the diseases on this planet."

"Just this morning you were whining about having nothing to do. Now you want to shoo away work."

"I'm not a missing-persons bureau. Why should I be made to suffer because some prepubescent was careless enough to misplace his own flesh and blood?"

"You don't know suffering. Try sitting around listening to you sigh and moan and cheat at Clue."

"I never cheat! It's not my fault Miss Scarlett would never choose a wrench to commit murder, with rat poison available at every True Value in Greater New York! Phooey!"

"Pfui!"

That never failed to derail one of his tantrums, the ability of seemingly everyone else in his orbit to pronounce Wolfe's favorite epithet without hosing down the room. Before he could fill the vacuum I said, "I'll bring the kid in. You want I should put down papers?"

The moon face turned red and screwed up, but instead of bawling, he said, "Remain standing, and be prepared to hurl yourself between us the moment he starts to sneeze. There are four million strains of bacilli on the head of a pin. I shudder to think how many are harbored in a child's nostrils."

❧

Jasper Hull turned the big globe with a palm in passing; Lyon sucked in air through his teeth. The kid stopped in front of his desk.

"You're fat."

"And you have no pubic hair. Please remove your cap. The room is heated sufficiently and the roof doesn't leak."

He uncovered a shock of red hair and hopped up onto the orange leather chair. "My mother's dead. I live with my aunt. She don't know I'm here. She says if my father was worth looking for he wouldn't have to be looked for."

"She has a point, though the syntax is dubious logically. Why do you want to find him?"

"Aunt Jill's okay, but I'm sick of living with girls. My father left before I was born. I'm not sure my mother even knew his name." He lifted his chin.

"That's unfortunate. Without a name or a description, there's no place to start."

"He's a tall skinny redhead and his name's William Thew."

I was taking notes, poised as ordered to throw myself into the bacterial breach if necessary. "That's T-H-E-W?"

"I don't know. He didn't spell it out."

Lyon said, "You stated he left before you were born. When did you meet?"

There was a tooth missing from Jasper's grin. "You figured that out from what I said."

"I'm fat, not a fool. Answer the question."

"It was the day my mother died, in Brooklyn General Hospital."

Kids are natural reporters; it's only when they grow up that they learn to digress and embellish. Jasper's mother had been hit by a truck in a crosswalk near their apartment six months ago and died a few days later without regaining consciousness. That day, the boy and his aunt got off the hospital elevator just as the man he'd described was leaving his mother's room. The man, who was about thirty, was wearing a heavy topcoat over faded jeans and was obviously not a hospital employee. Asked if he'd come to visit the patient, he'd said yes. When the aunt asked who he was, he'd hesitated, turned toward a window in the corridor, then turned back and said, "William Thew."

"How do you know my sister?"

"We, uh, went to school together."

"Is she awake?"

"No."

"It was very kind of you to come. Where can I contact you in case her condition changes?"

He gave her a phone number, then looked at his watch and said he had to get back to work. The elevator was open, and as he stepped inside, Jasper spoke up. "What kind of work?"

"I'm an artist." The doors slid shut and he descended.

"Did you have any contact after that?" Lyon asked.

"No. After Mom died, Aunt Jill tried the number, but it was phony. We looked for him at the funeral. He didn't show."

"How did he know your mother was in the hospital?"

"The accident was in the paper. He must've read about it."

"Did either of you ask at the nurses' station if he'd stopped there to find out what room she was in?"

"My aunt did, but you know what those places are like, nurses coming and going all the time. Nobody remembered him."

"What makes you think he's your father?"

"Well, we both have red hair."

"Ten percent of the population does."

"I just know, okay?"

"Not okay. Mr. Woodbine informed you I'm not a fortuneteller, and I don't believe you are one either."

"Aunt Jill thinks I'm nuts too. Gimme a pencil and a piece of paper."

Lyon looked at me. I got a sheet of stationery out of my desk and a Cross pen and gave them to the kid. He folded the paper into a stiff square, stuck his tongue out the corner of his mouth, and scribbled, stopping a couple of times to look up at Lyon. He handed back the sheet blank side up. I passed it to Lyon, who glanced at it and gave it back to me. I grinned. In a few strokes the kid had captured his basketball-shaped head and that sourpuss expression he wears when he thinks he's being poker-faced. Jasper Hull had a future as a cartoonist.

"He said he's an artist," Jasper said. "My mother couldn't draw a straight line and neither can my aunt. Where'd I get it if not from him?"

"Young man, Shakespeare's father was once fined for maintaining a dung heap in his front yard. His son wrote *Hamlet*. Gus!"

The kid jumped, but I was used to that bellow. The major-domo in the rusty cutaway coat hobbled in with a cream soda and left as Lyon pried loose the top, deposited it in his desk drawer, swigged from the can, and burped. Then he started digging in his ear with a finger.

That caught me off-guard. I hadn't thought the conversation had provided anything to bother waking up his cortex over.

"I can draw you a picture of Thew," Jasper said. "You could show it around, like they do on *Law & Order*."

But the excavation went on another minute without comment. Finally the finger was withdrawn. "Do you remember the number of your mother's room at Brooklyn General?"

"Six-oh-eight, why?"

"You came here seeking the services of a detective, not lessons in the practice of the craft. Please leave a number where you can be reached with Mr. Woodbine."

"What about that picture?"

"Young man, I have no intention of tramping all over the city asking strangers to look at a doodle, and Mr. Woodbine has far too many other responsibilities. Give him your number."

"Yeah, I bet he calls."

I showed him out and went back to the office, where Lyon was studying his portrait. "The tough little nut stole my pen," I said, "but that's all right. He sure can draw."

"Caricature is the lowest form of humor. Dispose of it."

I put it in my breast pocket. I hoped I could find a frame the right size.

"I want you to take the digital camera and photograph the view from all the windows between room six-oh-eight and the elevator in Brooklyn General," he said. "Shoot every angle."

"They'll think I'm a terrorist."

"Phooey. 'Hospital security' is a contradiction in terms. If he hadn't the ill fortune to encounter Jasper Hull and his aunt, William Thew would have been in and out like a ghost."

"Why ill fortune; child support?"

"Don't put the horse before the cart."

"I think you're supposed to."

"Pre–Industrial Age semantics. Thew hoards personal data as if it were gold, but I am an intellectual Jesse James. When he ran into Jill and Jasper, he wandered down my stagecoach road."

I got the camera out of the safe. "I'll hang on to a shot just to get one of you in the saddle. Tabloids'll eat it up."

❖

I didn't ask what was behind the assignment; he'd just have given me the speech about cadging lessons in the practice of the craft. I picked a quiet time during visiting hours and took thirty shots. There was just the one window in the corridor between 608 and the elevator, so it didn't take long, and I finished just before an orderly got off on that floor pushing his squeaky cart. I boarded the elevator with the camera tucked under my coat and found a one-hour place on Utica to make prints.

Ansel Adams wouldn't have gotten up to look at my portfolio: cars in the parking lot, a brick hardware building with some old advertising on it, an ancient tenement coming down, a new high-rise going up, and an enterprising vendor selling flowers from a sidewalk stand, a bane to the competition in the gift shop downstairs. But Lyon gave each print the close attention of a Renaissance expert studying a cache of Rembrandt drawings. Some he slid to one side after thirty seconds of scrutiny, others he bent over at his desk with a heavy brass-handled magnifying glass in his puffy pink fist. He kept returning to one in particular, then sat back and laid aside the glass.

"Tell me what you think."

I looked at it. It was one of the shots in which the old hardware building featured prominently. "Great composition. I owe it all to a guy I met doing a year and a day for taking pictures of naked ladies in a tanning parlor."

"The composition is hideous, but I didn't send you out on behalf of *Architectural Digest*. The focus is good. The leaves having fallen from the trees this time of year gave you a better perspective on the billboard that would have been possible six months ago, when Jasper Hull and his aunt visited his mother in the hospital."

The sign was painted directly on the brick wall of the hardware, possibly using the very product it advertised.

"'It Covers the World,'" I read. "And sure enough, there it is dumping out of a bucket all over terra firma, one coat. I bet Sherwin-Williams has been using that slogan for a hundred years."

Lyon drew a Sharpie from a squat toby mug of Napoleon on his desk and spent another minute bent over the picture. When he sat back, I saw that Jasper Hull had nothing on Claudius Lyon in the freehand-art department. He'd sketched a close approximation of bunches of maple leaves on the naked tree branches that had stood between the camera and its subject.

But it wasn't his technique that drew a long low whistle from me; much to the annoyance of Lyon, who when he condescends to purse his lips and blow, manages only a dry whoosh. His expression curdled further. "Indeed. Have we any friendly contacts on the police force?"

"Stoddard's as friendly as it gets, and you know where he'd admire to put his size thirteen."

I'm not without resources, however, and got a buddy on the staff of the *Habitual Handicapper* to call in a couple of markers in Records and Information downtown. When he checked in, Lyon eavesdropped on the extension. "Encouraging," he said when we hung up; which coming from him is a rave. "What is your reporter friend's name?"

"Radislav Kubelski." Noting his sour expression I added, "Sorry, boss. Archie Goodwin's got the market cornered on Lon Cohens."

"I don't know what you're talking about. Please telephone young Mr. Hull and arrange an appointment."

⚜

"Mr. Woodbine, I take it? I'm Jillian Hull."

Next to a full pardon from the governor it was the nicest surprise I could have hoped to find on the doorstep. She was on the bright side of thirty, a honey of a honey blonde with her hair pinned back loosely behind cute little ears and blue eyes as big as campaign buttons. She came up to my shoulder and I could've lifted her in one hand, but I didn't chance it. She wasn't smiling.

Neither was Jasper, slumped next to her with his fists in his pockets. "She was there when you called. She made me tell."

"My nephew's been through a traumatic time, Mr. Woodbine. Humoring him is one thing, taking advantage of his fantasies in a season of mourning quite another. It may even be criminal."

I leered; Goodwin grins, but my mouth doesn't work that way. The suit she wore fit her too well here and there to back up her pique. "Pardon my not responding, but it wouldn't be hospitable to make you go through it all again for Lyon. He's the criminal in charge. I'm just the henchman."

"Take me to him, please."

It being a few minutes short of evening business hours, I trotted upstairs and gave him the news in the plant room. He was up to his elbows in sheep manure, but it wasn't enough of a distraction to keep him from blushing. Nero Wolfe only distrusts the female sex; Claudius Lyon is terrified of it. "Tell her she isn't involved and turn her out."

"She'd take Jasper with her. He's a minor, she's his guardian. You'd be giving up your curtain-closer." Seeing that he was undecided, I added, "She thinks we're both criminals, which makes her half right. The odds are better than even she'll march straight to the cops, and you know what that means."

The prospect of another tense meeting with Stoddard made him forget himself. He rubbed his nose, leaving a stain. The whole world was going to stink now. "Seat her on the sofa, out of my direct line of sight."

"She already took the orange chair."

"Sweet Mr. Moto! They have the rest of the world; why must they lay siege to my one little corner?"

The doorbell rang. I went downstairs and took a slant through the trick window. The angular figure perched on the stoop sent me bounding back up to the plant room. "It's the captain."

"What captain?" He was busy disinfecting himself at the sink.

"Crunch, of course. He's doing a survey door-to-door on whether we eat his cereal with milk or straight from the box. Who else? Stoddard."

Lyon didn't blush this time; he whitened a shade. Authority of any kind always took the wind out of him. Me, too, but my reasons are well known. Maybe his old man had caught him filching candy when he was even littler than he was now and had a cop friend put him in the clink to teach him a lesson. They say that's how Hitchcock got started. "Word must have reached him of our inquiries," he squeaked. "Don't answer!"

"He'll just come back madder."

The ringing stopped and the banging started. Lyon bobbed his head, washing his hands furiously. "I suppose we must let him sit in, if only for the sake of the door."

"Got you, Woodbine," greeted Stoddard when I opened up. "Lyon too. Using police services for private business."

"Business involves statements and receipts and scratches in a ledger. This is a hobby. And police records are public property."

I'd cribbed the speech from Lyon. There was more to it, but a steel fist shot out of a coat sleeve and took up the slack in my windpipe. I squeaked—plagiarizing again from the boss.

I never found out how far he intended to take it, because Jillian and Jasper Hull came out of the office to see what all the noise was about. When Stoddard saw them his eyes returned to their sockets and he let go.

When I finished coughing I made introductions and told everyone what he and she needed to know to that point. We went into the office, where the captain commandeered the orange chair, leaving two of the smaller green ones for the other guests.

Promptly on the hour, the building shook from the elevator rattling in the shaft, but the effect of the maestro's big entrance was spoiled when it got stuck between the second and first floors. This had happened before, and there was only one way to jar it back into operation. He was loath to do it with an audience. However, after a moment of mulling, the thudding began; pictures danced on the walls, and anyone with half an imagination could picture the chunky little passenger jumping up and down in the car. Finally the mechanism kicked back in with a dry chuckle and the cage settled to ground level. Lyon emerged, vest, lapels, and pocket handkerchief in perfect alignment, but his face was as red as the fruit of the *Lycopersicum anormalus* in the pot he held in both hands.

Jasper stifled a snort as the host made his dignified waddle to his chair; it was the first time I'd seen the little squirt behave like a normal child.

When he was seated, Lyon nodded to each visitor, making eye contact with none. "Thank you for coming. The presence of Miss Hull and Mr. Stoddard is an unexpected pleasure, however uninvited."

The two thus named started to talk at the same time. Stoddard found his manners in some cluttered corner and shut his mouth. Jillian Hull said, "I'm glad the police are here. It will make it easier to prefer charges against you for swindling a minor."

"Mr. Stoddard investigates fraud, which, as he can tell you, requires an exchange of money. Young Master Hull will confirm that I've declined compensation of any kind."

Stoddard thumped the arm of his chair with a horned palm. "You don't have to, as long as you can get the police to do your work for free."

Lyon swallowed, stifling a squeak. "Hardly free. I pay confiscatory taxes that contribute in no small measure to your department's budget. The information I obtained there is community property and was connected only indirectly to my investigation. I conducted it merely to confirm my suspicions. Mr. Woodbine?"

I got up from my desk and handed Jasper the fax we'd received that day from NYPD Brooklyn.

"Is that the man you met in the hospital last spring?" Lyon asked.

The boy started bouncing in his seat; there was hope for him yet. "That's him! That's my father!" He gave it to his aunt, who looked up from it and nodded. "It looks like a mug shot," she said.

"It is. The man's name is Randolph Otto. Currently he's in the New York State Penitentiary in Ossining, serving a sentence of ten to fifteen years for burglary. It's his second offense."

"His name's William Thew." Jasper was sullen again.

"The name doesn't appear among his known aliases. I hardly expected it to." Lyon scowled at the plant on his desk and pinched a leaf, squashing a bug. He wiped his hand and returned the hanky to his pocket. "When you met, it was May, a particularly pleasant month this year. I suspected the man was there for no legitimate purpose when you told me he was wearing a heavy overcoat. In warm weather, bulky coats are useful for one thing only: concealing stolen items. Armed with that supposition, I turned to the police to determine whether they had investigated a complaint of plundering at Brooklyn General during that time. The news that a suspect had been arrested and convicted was a bonus. I congratulate your brother officers, Mr. Stoddard."

The captain said something inappropriate for a lady and child in the room, or for that matter my Uncle Burt. I'd have made an example of him if my throat weren't still sore.

"The late Ms. Hull—Jasper's mother—had nothing of value in her room," Lyon continued; "otherwise, I'm sure Jasper would have noted that something was missing and included that fact when he reported the events of that day to me. Mr. Otto left her room empty-handed."

Jillian said, "I'd brought home her personal effects the day before. She wasn't expected to recover, and I've heard stories about watches and purses disappearing from hospital rooms." She didn't elaborate. Apparently she hated to interrupt his story, however briefly.

"A footpad, surprised in the midst of his pillaging, will say anything to deflect suspicion long enough for him to make his escape. Unfortunately, Jillian Hull assisted him unwarily by asking if he was there to visit her sister. He seized upon that, and when she asked his name, he gave her the first thing that suggested itself."

Jasper hadn't given up yet. "That don't make sense! He could've said Tom Smith or John Jones. How do you come up with William Thew out of nowhere?"

"You don't. When you said he'd looked out the window before identifying himself, I decided to send Mr. Woodbine to Brooklyn General to photograph the view through the window."

I was still standing. He opened his top drawer and handed me two of the pictures I'd taken. I gave one to Jasper. It was one of the shots of the advertisement painted on the wall of the brick hardware building. The legend read:

SHERWIN-WILLIAMS PAINT
It Covers the World!

An illustration accompanied it, showing a can of paint spilling its contents onto the globe.

"I don't get it." The boy passed the photo to his aunt, who looked at it, then at Lyon with her eyebrows lifted.

Lyon said, "The conditions were somewhat different from when Randolph Otto looked out on the same scene. It was spring, as I said, and tree leaves obscured parts of the sign. I've created an amateur artist's rendition of the scene as it would have appeared to him. Arnie?" The fat little exhibitionist was excited, I could tell; he forgot to address me formally in company only when he could barely contain himself.

I handed Jasper the picture Lyon had doctored with his Sharpie, blacking out the portions that would have been covered by leaves:

WILLIAM
the W

The boy looked up, his pinched little face pale. "He said he was an artist!"

"Inspiration from the same source. An artist uses paint. He wasn't your father. At the time you were born, he'd been in prison in New Jersey for more than a year. That was his first offense."

Stoddard snatched the photo from Jillian, flung it to the floor, hurled himself at Lyon's desk, and brought him up to date on his opinion of word puzzles and Lyon himself. He laid a blazing trail to the exit, leaving Lyon white and shaken. Jasper wasn't any more pleased, but his aunt restrained him from kicking a chair and thanked Lyon for putting an end to the business. She was a pretty good sport. I wondered how she felt about semi-reformed felons.

Lyon handed her an envelope from his drawer. It bore his letterhead and a name addressed in his childlike hand.

"It isn't sealed," she said.

"I wouldn't presume. As the boy's guardian you'd naturally want to know what it contained before you delivered it."

She left, resting a hand on one of Jasper's hunched shoulders. Lyon and I spent the rest of the evening quietly, he reading the Hardy Boys in an E. Phillips Oppenheim dust jacket, I making marks in the *Habitual Handicapper*; a two-year-old named Brushstroke was running in the third at Belmont. I didn't tell the boss I'd caught a glimpse of the name he'd scribbled on the envelope, and when

I found out later it belonged to the director of an art scholarship program at Brooklyn College, I didn't tell him that. The program had been endowed by an anonymous benefactor. Nothing about it sounds the least bit typical of Lyon's role model. I figure I'll needle him with it when I frame and hang Jasper's caricature of him.

Which I may not for a while. Today at lunch, Claudius Lyon leaned on his elbow and held up a tired-looking lox drooping on the end of his fork.

"Arnie," he said, "how long have you been working for me?"

WOLFE AT THE DOOR

"These fisticuffs by proxy will be the death of our civilization."

Apart from having a name that sounded like billiard balls colliding on green felt, Heinrich Knicknacker didn't come off as the sort that indulged in recreation, or for that matter any pastime that passed time to no profit. He was a tall scarecrow type that didn't dress like one, with a bony face and a wheat-colored crop of Uncle Sam chin whiskers under a Homburg hat. His double-breasted blue suit with gold buttons gave him a military air and he held his gold-knobbed stick at shoulder-arms position.

"You are *Herr* Lyon, no?" he greeted.

I said, "That's right."

"*Herr* Lyon, I am Heinrich Knicknacker." His *a*'s were short and he coughed his *k*'s. I thought he was hawking up a cat.

"You misunderstood. You said I am *Herr* Lyon, no, and I confirmed the analysis. I am *Herr* Woodbine, yes. I answer the door for *Herr* Lyon when Gus is absent." One more *Herr* and I'd need to dive into the throat spray.

He adjusted the monocle he wasn't wearing. "Who is this Gus?"

"The major-domo, and also the best kosher chef in Brooklyn. Currently the second best in Westport, Connecticut, where he's visiting his brother, who's the best there. That may not be fair to Gus, though, as you can swing a two-pound brisket anywhere in that state and not graze anyone remotely Jewish. Meanwhile we're dining on sardines and cream soda. Would you care to join us?"

"I would not. I seek consultation with Claudius Lyon."

"In that case you'll have to wait ten minutes. He's finishing dinner, if you want to call it that."

That was acceptable, and I hung up his hat and showed him into the front room, which is a reasonable enough facsimile of Nero Wolfe's front room in his Manhattan brownstone, given that Archie Goodwin, the man who answers the door for Wolfe when Fritz, Wolfe's Gus, is absent, has never provided specific details about its appointments in his accounts of his employer's affairs. Claudius Lyon, who's dedicated his adult life to duplicating Wolfe's, had spent many hours poring over the record with that result, so his decorator had had carte blanche with chinoiserie and chintz. Personally I thought it looked like the cabin of a junk sinking in Beijing harbor, if it has one; but since I'd split a seventy-five markup on the materials with the decorator I kept my trap shut.

I reported to the dining room, where the little meatball was indeed forking sardines straight from the can and washing them down with the sticky beverage he prefers to Wolfe's beer.

"Send him away. My digestion is in sufficient distress without entertaining guests. I yearn for Gus's matzo."

"He looks like money."

"Phooey. I'm made of money."

"Also lard, but it's your money Nathaniel Parker's interested in. You need liquid funds to blitz him at the start."

He chewed on that along with a mouthful of greasy fish. Parker, who represented Nero Wolfe in all things legal, had written Lyon recently, demanding he cease and desist his imitation of Parker's client immediately or face a civil suit for identity theft. We were sure that Captain Stoddard, Lyon's nemesis in the Brooklyn Police Department, had put the bug in Wolfe's ear. Practicing private investigation without a license irked him in general, but he'd made nailing Lyon a personal crusade.

But my little speech of encouragement was a waste of time, bigger than and almost as fat as the man I worked for. Unlike his lazy idol, Lyon never passed up an opportunity to act like a genuine detective; but he paid me to pretend to have to prod him, because that's what Archie Goodwin did for the man *he* worked for. If it weren't for spending my days off bribing jockeys at the track for inside information, that sanity, I'd be as bananas as the boss.

"Very well, I'll see him, but only as a distraction from this nuisance. He may be a police plant to entice me into accepting payment for my services, leading to my arrest."

That surprised me on two counts. First, the only "plant" I expected him to recognize was the tomato variety, which he cultivates in place of the notable Nero's more challenging orchids; second, because as the only official crook in residence I should have been the one to suspect Stoddard's sneaky hand. Lyon's amateur status protects him from prosecution, but Stoddard isn't above entrapment, or for that matter thumbscrews. With Lyon in the jug, I'd have to go back to stealing from strangers. The cook at Sing Sing hasn't Gus's way with a blintz.

Ten minutes later, when Lyon was swinging his heels above the floor in the overstuffed throne behind his cruiser-class desk (everything in the office was built to Nero Wolfe's much larger scale, making its occupant look even more like a member of the Lollipop Guild than had nature herself), I plopped Heinrich Knicknacker into the orange leather chair reserved for VIPs. He got right down to business in Prussian fashion.

"I own a chain of German restaurants on the East Coast. Last year I went into semiretirement and placed my nephew, Oscar, in charge, purely in a management capacity; I maintain controlling interest. Now he wishes to have me declared mentally incompetent so he can inherit right away."

Lyon asked him the terms of his will.

"It is a short document. Oscar is the sole beneficiary. He is all the family I have."

"Have your lawyer draw up a new will. Leave your estate to a favorite employee or the charity of your choice."

"I have thought of this, but my attorney informs me that if my nephew succeeds in his aim, any new will would be thrown out of court on the grounds of—I forget the phrase."

"Diminished capacity," I said. "I tried the same scam on my old man, but he turned me over to the cops on a separate matter before I could have the papers drawn up."

Knicknacker looked for explanation to Lyon, who scowled at me like a gassy baby. "Mr. Woodbine has an adolescent sense of humor. Are you incompetent, Mr. Knicknacker?"

"I most certainly am not." He pointed his chin whiskers square at his interrogator.

"What, then, has your nephew to offer as evidence?"

"Memory lapse. He overheard me during a telephone conversation and claims that in the middle of it I forgot who I was addressing."

"What was the conversation?"

"I would rather not say."

Lyon moved the potted *Lycopersicon hybridum* on his desk to give him a straight shot at the speaker. Since a quadriplegic can grow a tomato just by ignoring it, that was as much exercise as he'd take all day. "A wise man once said no one can prove a negative," he said. "He might have added that it's even less possible when the subject won't cooperate. Arnie?"

I looked at him dumbly. He kept jerking his head leftward. I thought it was a seizure. Finally I put down my notebook, got up from my chair, and asked him in a low voice if he needed an ambulance.

"Don't you know a signal when you see one?" he whispered.

"Signal?"

"Hat! Hat!"

When I realized it wasn't an asthmatic attack either, I went out and retrieved Knicknacker's Homburg from the foyer. I tried to hold it out like Gus in his best servant's mode, but I must have looked like a haberdasher, because Uncle Heinrich kept staring at it without recognition. I wondered if his bean was actually beyond its sell-by date, as his nephew insisted.

"Good day, sir," Lyon said. "I am not semiretired, and haven't time to waste."

Which was a bluff. He'd had his successes, but Americans being Americans, a man who offers his service gratis is generally regarded to be charging exactly what they're worth. Lyon's legal trouble was only part of the reason for his bad cess; how could he ape his hero's sleuthing prowess with nothing to sleuth?

The gambit worked. Knicknacker sat flexing and unflexing his bony fingers on the knob of his stick, then acknowledged defeat with a nod.

"I have a weakness," he confessed. "Not a serious one, but I enjoy making wagers on sports events. Can you assure me this conversation will be kept in confidence?"

Lyon nodded in turn, playing accordion with his many chins. "In this I have an advantage over other private inquiry agents, who can't shield themselves behind the seal of attorney-client privilege in a court of law. I have no license to place in jeopardy."

"And *Herr* Woodbine?"

"Mr. Woodbine is merely contrary. I trust him with my secrets if not my silver."

I put indignation on my face, but it was halfhearted. Having no character I consider myself a fair judge of one, but I'd fumbled when I'd piped our potential client as a man who had no truck with games and such. I couldn't remember spotting him at any of the bookmaking operations in my circuit.

"I accept your assurances. At the time Oscar came in on my end of the telephone conversation, I was having a heated difference of opinion with my, er, contact man. He persisted in saying that all five of the football games I had bet upon had gone against me, but I reminded him that it was four only. I had placed a substantial sum on the fifth, and my team had managed to cover the spread."

"Do you remember all the games at issue? Arnie?"

I was ahead of him, seated at my desk with my hands on the computer keyboard. Lyon fills his many leisure hours reading whodunits, not watching sports; he sneaks the stories into his plant room when he wants everyone to think he's monkeying with his beefsteaks and Romas. He wouldn't know the Packers from Pittsburgh. Without hesitating, the well-dressed scarecrow remembered all the games and which teams he'd bet on. That worked in favor of his story; a loser has to be pretty far off the beam to forget where his money went.

"When did these contests take place?" asked Lyon.

"Last Sunday."

The fat water rat looked to me for confirmation. He's convinced that shiftless types like me fritter away the Lord's day casting their ill-gotten lots on such ephemera, and know all the results by heart. He's right, but I confirmed them anyway just to shake up his low opinion. Like his role model, he keeps a backlog of newspapers in a cabinet, but unlike Archie Goodwin, I'm always getting them out of order, looking up lottery numbers and tracking old friends' fortunes in the police columns. At length I found last Sunday's sports section and turned to the box scores.

"Check, including the one he says he picked right." I didn't add that I'd been way off on that one. It had cost Lyon his mother's Limoges, but I hoped to get it out of hock after Saturday's trifecta.

"Who won the argument?" Lyon asked.

"*Du lieber Gott*, who else? The con—*Ach!* The bookie. He'd written it down wrong when I placed the bet, but to whom can I complain, the Better Business Bureau?" Knicknacker thumped the floor with his stick.

"You said your nephew accused you of forgetting who was on the other end of the conversation. Is that at all likely?"

"If it were, I would indeed be guilty of losing my reason. Who could forget such an exchange?"

"As you say, one whose grasp upon reality is tenuous. What were you saying when he overheard you?"

"I was shouting that the man was mistaken, that one of the teams I'd chosen had won. I leave it to you to determine how Oscar could possibly have interpreted that to mean I assumed I was speaking to emergency services."

"Is that what he said?"

"He bounded into my office and seized me by the shoulders, as if he feared I might collapse. He told me to lie down until help came. I never realized he was so good an actor. I asked him what on earth he was talking about. That's when he told me. I said, 'Has everyone but me lost his mind?' and thrust the receiver into his hand. When he confirmed who it was I'd been talking to, he appeared even more upset. That was when he suggested I was slipping."

Forgetfulness was contagious that day. Lyon started to shout for Gus, then remembered and asked me to bring him a cream soda. He offered refreshment to our guest, who shook his head. Recounting the details of the encounter with his nephew had brought color to his knobby cheeks.

When I came back with the can, Knicknacker was answering another question.

"*Ich kann nicht.* He has taken no legal measures that I am aware of. But it is only a matter of time. Why else would he fabricate such a monstrous story? I admit we have never been close; his late father and I were far apart in age, and I saw him little until he graduated from college with a business degree and came to me looking for an executive position. By the time I decided to slow down, he'd earned promotion to general manager. I suspect he's afraid I'll gamble away his inheritance if left to my own devices, ridiculous improbability that it is. The only other explanation is ruthless ambition on his part."

"What do you wish me to do?"

"Prove to him his plan is doomed to fail, that my mind is sound and that all this play-acting is a waste of time."

Lyon shook his head carefully; the jiggling of his cheeks distracts him.

"That's work for a psychiatrist, and even his findings would be subject to interpretation in court."

"Discover, then, the source of his suspicion. He must have some reason to believe he can twist the law in his favor."

"That would require interviewing the other two witnesses to your telephone conversation. I've heard your side, and I know your nephew's, so nothing can be gained by questioning him. What is the name of your bookie?"

"He would be upset if I identified him for a stranger. His is not a legitimate enterprise."

"Mr. Woodbine is not unfamiliar with the betting world. I could instruct him to place some calls, but that would take time, and if you're right about Oscar's motives, give him opportunity to prepare a case against you. If he is to be dissuaded, we must act swiftly."

"I am sorry, but I cannot divulge the information."

Lyon squeaked; an exasperated little noise he sometimes makes that sounds like a mouse passing wind. "You have presented me with an impossible challenge, sir."

"You cannot help me?"

"I did not say that; merely that the challenge is impossible. Come back tomorrow and I will answer that question."

I took Knicknacker's hat from my desk and saw him to the front stoop. He leaned heavily on his stick, a defeated man, as he descended to the sidewalk. I kept watch in case he decided to collapse, and was rewarded for my good Samaritanship when an unmarked police cruiser parked at the curb growled its siren and an unwelcome head poked out the window on the passenger's side. Captain Stoddard showed the old German his shield. They were too far away for eavesdropping, but when I saw the cop's nasty little smile I knew he'd heard something he thought he could use. I ducked back inside as Knicknacker walked away, just in case Stoddard saw me and decided to arrest me for loitering or breathing the same air as an honest citizen.

Lyon took the bad news with a shudder, then a sigh. "He has nothing for leverage. Knicknacker and I did not discuss payment."

"You're forgetting he's a two-trick pony these days," I said. "He'll go straight to Nero Wolfe with the news you're using his act to drum up business, ignoring Lawyer Parker's cease-and-desist letter. He'll take you to court. Goodwin, probably, will just beat the stuffing out of me."

"That, at least, would be direct and honorable. These fisticuffs by proxy will be the death of our civilization. The fall of Rome and the rise of the legal profession were not simultaneous by coincidence. What is your opinion of our client's state of mind?"

"Sure, we might as well kill time while waiting for the process server. The old fellow's almost as unlucky as me, but when it comes to marbles I'd say he's got all he started out with. I guess it wouldn't be the first time a bookie failed at taking dictation, but this one's lucky he wasn't doing business with Moe the Moose. Should I start calling around?"

"Would it do any good?"

"Probably not. The ones I know don't hash over their relationships with other customers."

He swigged cream soda, giving himself a frothy mustache, and opened his belly drawer to drop the pull-tab inside among the others. Either he did that to keep track of his consumption, the way Wolfe counted beer bottle caps, or he was saving up to make a chainlink fence; which by now would reach clear around the block. "We have no choice, then, but to discover the answer in what Knicknacker told us."

"Lots of luck with that. How does an argument over a bet turn into a nine-one-one call?"

He responded to that, after a beat, by plugging one ear with an index finger. That tore it for me. It was a gesture he saved for just as he was about to lift the cover off a serving tray and reveal the Hope Diamond, but this time he had to be bluffing.

Unless our client had told him something I'd missed while I was out getting his can of carbonated diabetes. If Lyon was holding out on me, all the hot air he was always blowing about fair play in detective stories was as phony as his Nero Wolfe act.

The doorbell rang. When I answered it, a squirt in a stiff new pair of overalls held up a flat plastic tray filled with miniature tomato plants. "Delivery for Claudius Lyon. He has to sign for it in person."

"Bull." I put the door in his face.

When he rang again I slid the chain on and peered out.

"Where'd I go wrong?" he asked.

"The costuming. Next time throw the overalls in a washer and then roll around in the dirt for a half-hour before you come calling. You must think I never stuck out my hand for the Irish Sweepstakes and brought it back holding a piece of paper that said *The State of New York v. Arnie Woodbine*."

"Hey, I just got the job. I made the plant store just before it closed."

"Hand it off to someone else. Tell Nathaniel Parker that Lyon's harder to serve than Howard Hughes."

"Hughes is dead."

"What'd I say?" I put the door back in his face.

I returned to the office to tell Lyon the wheels of justice were grinding faster than usual, but he was still petting his brain with his finger.

The more I went over what I'd heard in that office, the more sure I was that whatever Knicknacker had said that would explain the misunderstanding with his nephew had taken place outside my hearing, and the more sure I was of that, the madder I got. I'd a good mind to pull a Goodwin and threaten to quit, but he might take me up on it, and then where'd I be? In my parole cop's office, trying to talk him out of sending me back up for lack of gainful employment.

So I steamed for two hours, during which time I turned away a tall party in a FedEx uniform, a pamphlet pusher in a blue suit and horn-rim glasses, and a kid looking for a lost dog. The kid at least might have been legit, but if I saw the dog I'd probably have booted it in the keister. Lyon was still foraging when I put out my desk lamp and went up to bed.

⚜

He woke me on the house phone the next morning. I reported to his bedroom and found him sitting up in his Olympic-sized canopy bed in green silk pajamas, munching Ding Dongs from the emergency stash in his nightstand. He had on the angry-infant scowl he wore when Gus wasn't around to schmear his bagels and deliver them on a tray. "Call Knicknacker and arrange for his presence after I come down from the plant room."

"You pulled it out of your ear finally? When?"

"I wasn't looking at the clock, but I can tell you when the first glimmer came."

"Sure. When I wasn't there to see it myself."

"Phooey. It was something *you* said. What the devil was all that bell-ringing about last night?"

"Hobbits with summonses. What do you mean, something *I* said?"

He poked a whole chocolate hockey puck into his mouth, ignoring me. Marooned in that huge bed wearing that bilious sleep suit from the Husky section of FAO Schwartz, he looked like a chubby leprechaun with the sniffles. "Do you suppose Gus would be upset if I ordered hasenpfeffer from Knicknacker's restaurant chain?"

"I wouldn't risk it. He might tear up the bill, and Stoddard would consider that a form of payment."

He changed the subject again. "Make a note to call Parker when this business is finished. Surely a man who represents Nero Wolfe understands the sanctity of a man's home."

"Why don't you call Wolfe himself?"

His expression told me that any such direct contact would cause the universe to fold in on itself. "No, no, no. Call Parker."

⚜

The doorbell rang while Lyon was up fussing with his vines, too early for our client. On my way to answer it I selected a Louisville Slugger from the umbrella stand, strictly to discourage any more paperhangers; a golem like Stoddard would have bitten it in two and performed a colonoscopy on me with the pieces. But the man on the stoop looked too respectable for a sneak and too *Homo sapiens* for the captain, in an oyster-colored suit and a tie to match. He was clean-shaven, in his twenties, but I saw a family resemblance in the bony planes of his face.

"Oscar Knicknacker, I presume?" I lowered the bat.

"Are you Lyon?" He used his chin for a pointer just like Heinrich, but the effect was different without the wiry tuft of hair.

"Hang on while I take six inches off my legs and put ten around my belly. Until then the name is Woodbine."

"Take me to him."

I asked if he knew anything about gardening.

"Gardening? Certainly not. I'm in the restaurant business."

"Then no can do. Apart from me, Mr. Lyon only lets plant people into his plant room. So far, none has asked for an invitation.

Come back in an hour and I'll see if I can get you an appointment."
I started to close the door.

He stuck a foot inside the threshold. "I demand to see him. My
uncle told me he hired him to interfere with my concerns for his
health. His condition will deteriorate without treatment."

"So will this one." I lifted the bat, brought it down with great
determination on his instep, and shut the door while he was howling
and hopping around holding the foot.

I went up to the greenhouse. Lyon, wearing a black rubber
apron, neoprene gauntlets, black goggles, and a facemask, was
spraying a display of green orbs with an old-fashioned pump
gun; he was convinced that some rock-climbing strain of bug had
penetrated Brooklyn and scaled his townhouse to the roof, but the
only thing there resembling an insect was the master of the house
in his HAZMAT getup. Of course, it was all just an excuse to
buy more plant stuff and take up the prescribed four hours daily
with a strain of fauna that required nothing much more than sun
and solitude. The owner of the local gardening shop had put his
daughter through medical school entirely on Lyon's tab. And they
say *I* take unfair advantage of his fruitcakery.

He stopped spraying long enough to hear my report, delivered
through a handkerchief, then laid down a fresh noxious yellow
cloud. "If the nephew comes back, show him into the office. He
might as well hear what I have to say."

"I fetched him a pretty good clout on a gunboat. He might have
a lawyer with him. They're coming in swarms now. If I were you I'd
carry that bug bomb with me everywhere I went."

⚜

Oscar came limping back without benefit of counsel. When I
opened the door, he drew back, but when I showed him my empty

palms he let me escort him, limping, to Lyon's brain box. I steered him away from the orange chair and into one of the green ones. "Refreshment? Coffee? Juice? Bengay?"

He was arranging his mouth into a suitably tart reply when another visitor arrived. The old German had changed into a gray suit, as military in appearance as the blue, but when he handed me his hat I saw his hair was uncombed and he gave the stick a good workout on the way to the office. If this kind of thing kept up, it would be crutches all around.

He stopped when he saw his nephew. "I won't share a room with this ungrateful little—"

"Uncle!" Oscar struggled to rise.

"Don't call me that. As far as I am concerned we are strangers."

"Opposite corners, pugs." I shoved the orange chair against the back of Heinrich's legs, folding him into it.

That took the starch out of him. He looked up pathetically. "I hope Lyon has good news."

"Me too. I can tell you he doesn't have any wax left in his right ear."

The dance card was full when the doorbell went off again, so I had my anti-process-server device in hand when I answered it. But I'd have preferred one of the pests to the tall, rangy beast of prey that stood there. "Get rid of that baseball bat before I shove it down your throat."

My idea had been more original, but I said, "Yes, Captain," and got rid of it.

"I followed your client here. You know I like to sit in on these little klatches of yours, just to make sure Lyon hasn't gone professional."

I didn't show him in, but only because he loped on ahead with me skulking at his heels. Some cops you can banter with and slide by. This one could take the starch out of a rice paddy.

I was at my desk, enjoying the uncomfortable silence, when the elevator shuddered down the shaft and the host came in, carrying the tomato du jour, and set the pot on his desk. He'd changed out of the *Ghostbusters* gear into a suit from the Portly Dwarf in Queens, but he trailed a strong scent of malathion. He blanched when he saw Stoddard, looking more volatile than usual in one of the green chairs; he considered the orange one his by right of conquest, but even he wasn't mean enough to dump an old man out of it; not, anyway, after he'd had his first gallon of coffee.

"You can flush the introductions," he said. "I just met the youngster, and Heiny and I are old friends from last night. Go ahead and hang yourself. Our mutual friend in Manhattan will be interested in hearing the details of your latest knockoff."

Lyon said, "I prefer the term *hommage*"; but his voice squeaked as he hopped up onto his big swivel.

"Gentlemen—" He cleared his throat, without altering the loose fan-belt effect. I took pity on him and fetched him a cream soda to soak away the parch. He drank off half and burped discreetly into a green handkerchief, then blew his nose. In a stronger voice: "To recap: Mr. Knicknacker the elder has accused Mr. Knicknacker the younger of scheming to wrest hold of his inheritance by having his uncle declared legally incompetent. The incident—"

"That's not true!" Oscar pointed his chin. "He suffers memory lapses. He needs supervision for his own safety."

"Lapses, plural? I was told there was only one such in question."

"I observed one only, yes, but the severity of it suggests the probability of others."

"One swallow does not make a summer. Your uncle explained that you overheard a telephone conversation he was having with the man who accepts his wagers on sporting contests, in the midst of which your uncle said something that led you to believe he'd forgotten to whom he was speaking. Is that correct as you remember the incident?"

"Yes. He seemed suddenly to think that he was talking to an emergency operator. Naturally, I assumed he was having some kind of episode, but when I expressed alarm—"

"Glee, you mean."

"Mr. Knicknacker." Lyon stilled the old man with a finger, saw he was still holding the handkerchief, and stuffed it back into his pocket.

"I was concerned," Oscar continued, "and became even more so when it developed that he hadn't been addressing who he thought he was. At that point he became extremely agitated, accusing me of conspiring against him. The doctor I turned to for advice informed me that paranoia is a common symptom of dementia. I want Uncle Heinrich to see this doctor. I have no designs on his money."

"That is good, because you will not get it, before my death *or* after." Heinrich seemed about to say more, but at a glare from Lyon gripped the knob of his stick in sullen silence.

"Both your uncle and yourself say that you thought he was calling emergency services. He used those words, 'emergency services'?"

"Of course not. That's too much of a mouthful in an urgent situation. He was shouting, 'Nine-one-one!' What was I supposed to think?"

"Liar!"

Lyon interjected. "Mr. Knicknacker. Heinrich. What was passing between you and your bookie at the precise moment Oscar entered your office? Please try to quote the exchange as accurately as possible."

He stroked his goat's whiskers. "He said, 'Pay up. Every one of your picks lost.' I said that was untrue."

"You said, quote, 'That was untrue'?"

"*Ach*, no. I see what you mean. Of course I would have said that in present tense. 'That is untrue.' But now that I think about it, what my actual words were, 'No, one of them won.'"

"Pardon me for belaboring this point. I've observed during conversation that when you become upset you revert to your native language. Yesterday, for example, when I asked who had won the argument with the bookie, you replied, '*Du lieber Gott*, who else? The bookie.' Roughly translated, the phrase means, 'For the love of God.'"

"*Ja*. I mean yes. I was a very young man when I emigrated from the shadow of the wall in Berlin, and I have worked hard to assimilate. Some situations, however, are too much for my adopted language to contain."

"Then it is possible, even probable, that you experienced a similar—lapse—during the altercation on the telephone?"

"I did, now that you jog my memory. When he said that every single one of my picks had lost, I said—"

Suddenly all the color drained from his bony features. "*Himmel!* Can it be?"

Lyon drained his can and burped again, this time with satisfaction. "'*Nein*,' you said. 'One won.'"

Heinrich Knicknacker shook his head slowly. "Not said. Shouted. I must have sounded like a maniac."

"Nine-one-one," I said. "Son of a—"

Oscar turned his head. "Uncle, I'm so sorry. There's nothing wrong with your mind."

The old man's face was grave. "Yes, there is. I allowed it to jump to an evil conclusion." He reached across the arm of his chair and patted his nephew's knee. Looking at our host: "Thank you, *Herr* Lyon. You have restored to me my flesh and blood."

Stoddard, sympathetic as ever to a warm family moment, exploded from his seat with an oath. "I'm going to enjoy watching the bloodsuckers drain you in court." He stamped out.

"Unpleasant man." But Lyon was bouncing his heels against his chair like a fat little boy with a Popsicle.

❧

We had cornflakes for dinner, but even that sacrifice wasn't enough to sour his mood. As we cleared the table—me stacking bowls and glasses and balancing them from palms to elbows, he carrying a spoon—Lyon said, "Again, Arnie, I must credit you for setting me on the right path, however unintentionally. When you referred to our magnificently efficient system of emergency public assistance by its universal telephone number, I realized the implications, particularly when the German tongue is involved. I'd consider raising your salary if you weren't already helping yourself to the household accounts."

I almost dropped a hundred clams in porcelain and crystal.

After ditching it all on the drain board in the kitchen, I followed him out into the hall, fit to express myself appropriately in high dudgeon, when a wide shadow blocked the dusky light coming in through the window in the front door.

"When you're through preening," I said, "you might try considering the implications of that lawsuit. I wouldn't put it past Nero Wolfe to fire his flunkies and serve you the papers himself."

"Phooey. Wolfe never leaves his house on business."

"But isn't identity theft personal?"

The doorbell rang.

WOLFE ON THE ROOF

*"My dear young lady, you need an advice columnist,
not a detective."*

Lyon was angry; I think.

You never can tell whether the little butterball is seriously miffed or just emulating Nero Wolfe, his role model and life's obsession.

Then again, it might have been disgruntlement over having to spend two hours playing with his tomatoes, which never need more than ten minutes' attention even in crisis; orchids are another thing, but tending to them is beyond his green thumb, which was not so green as the dress shirt he wore under his apron but almost as fat as his torso.

Too bad. If you're going to keep a greenhouse on your roof instead of a swell patio, you reap what you sow.

But he may just have been primping for our guest, whose Prada bag and Chanel suit indicated money, and whose blond head suggested the opportunity of my selling her the Triborough Bridge. She'd arrived unannounced, but I didn't want to risk alienation by asking her to wait, and as anyone knows who knows even one-tenth of what Claudius Lyon knows about Wolfe, nothing is more vexing to a fat genius detective than entertaining a client in his plant rooms.

"I cannot help you now, Miss—?"

"Alexandra Pring."

"I hope to cross this plum with that beefsteak, and create a tomato that is both delectable and substantial. If you wish to consult me, you must wait until eleven o'clock, when I'll speak with you in my office. Mr. Woodbine knows that, but has chosen to ignore the rules of this house." He favored me with the gassy-baby's face he thought petulant.

The fake. He was tickled pink over having a client. The one thing he can't pull off about his masquerade is a convincing show of pique at the chance to flash his brain before an audience. Since he's a rotten horticulturist, and can burn a salad in the kitchen, solving mysteries is the only thing he has left.

"But it can't wait! I've lost my job, and my rent is past due. Please make an exception this one time!"

I was batting only 500. I'm sure there are plenty of blond PhDs, but I'd sized this one up right. I flied out on the rest. In bright sunlight, the bag and suit were knockoffs; and now I was the one who was miffed.

Lyon hid his delight under a gruff litany of made-up Latin, fingering ordinary vines while drawing her out on the reason for her visit.

"I run errands for an eccentric millionaire in Queens," she said. "That is, I did. He was always complaining that he couldn't reach me because I keep forgetting to charge my cell." She opened the phony bag and showed him a cheap no-contract phone. "I admit I'm absent-minded. I keep forgetting to pay my rent, and by the time I think about it, the money's spent. But I'm very efficient once I'm given an errand. Mr. Quilverton must know that."

"Ronald Quilverton, of the Boston Quilvertons?" I perked up. There might be money in the thing after all, if she was as reliable as she claimed and Quilverton was grateful to have her back.

"Yes. I said he's eccentric. That's why he lives in Queens, New York, instead of on Beacon Hill back home."

Lyon scowled in earnest, wiping black loam onto his apron.

"The solution is hardly worthy of my abilities, Miss Pring. Tie a string to your finger, and remember to plug in your mobile."

"I've thought of that, of course. But how can I correct my behavior if my former employer won't take my calls asking for a second chance?"

"My dear young lady, you need an advice columnist, not a detective."

"Hear me out, please. The last time I spoke with him, I was walking down Junction. He was giving me an assignment when my phone beeped, warning me my battery had run out and the call was about to be dropped. He heard it. What I can't figure out is why he said what he said then."

"If it was 'You're fired,' I think I can educate you."

"'Steak and eggs.'"

"Once again?"

"I'm quoting. Well, I lost the signal before the second *s*, but it was definitely 'Steak and egg,' and of course no one says it that way in a restaurant, even if all he wants is one egg. What did he mean?"

"He was instructing you to bring him breakfast."

"Mr. Quilverton is a vegan. He wouldn't touch either item with a ten-foot fork.

"I tried calling him back from a landline, but he never answered. Maybe he had a stroke. I'd call nine-one-one, but if I'm wrong, he'd never forgive the intrusion. I'm as worried about him as I am about myself. He's a recluse and lives alone; he may be lying on his floor, with no one to help."

"'Steak and egg'; you're sure?"

"Yes."

I was thinking the eccentric was just plain nuts when Lyon surprised me by foraging in one ear with a finger. That was his answer to Wolfe's puckering his lips in and out, indicating he was near a solution. Either that or the food talk had him thinking about lunch.

"Miss Pring," he said, wiping wax onto his apron. "Did it occur to you Mr. Quilverton was imploring you not to think about a hearty morning meal, but to stay connected?"

"Stay connect—? Oh!"

"We're increasingly an aural society. 'Steak and eggs' and 'Stay connected,' the latter cut off abruptly when your cell lost power, would sound identical."

She pouted. "But I'm still out of a job." Then she brightened. "Perhaps—"

"No. Bringing a woman into this household would be like—" For once, the vocabulary he'd filched from Nero Wolfe failed him.

"Like crossing a plum with a beefsteak," I suggested.

WOLFE TRAP

"Season's greetings, Captain."

When you looked in the dictionary under "tough cop," you never got as far as the picture, because Captain Stoddard of the Brooklyn Bunco Squad would tear out the page and shove it down your throat.

So when I saw that craggy, bitter-almond face through the two-way glass in the front door of Claudius Lyon's brownstone I knew the day could only get better from there.

Turned out I was wrong.

"I know you're in there, Woodbine. That little gob of goo never leaves the place and you're too busy bleeding him dry to go out for a pint of Old Overshoe."

"One moment, please." I skedaddled to report the glad tidings to my employer.

He was sitting in the overstuffed green chair that was too big for him behind the desk that was too big for even Nero Wolfe, his hero and role model in the office he'd copied from a photo spread on Wolfe's place of business in *Knickerbocker*. I caught him reading Encyclopedia Brown before he could stash it behind a hefty copy of *Crime and Punishment*. The short fat faker never gave up the ruse.

He squeaked, turned a paler shade of boiled turnip, and said, "We don't have to let him in, do we? He doesn't have a warrant or anything, does he?"

"I couldn't tell from just his face. I don't think even a police dog like him goes around carrying them in his mouth."

"Tell him to go away." He reburied his nose in his book.

"Not me, boss. I'd sooner punch a grizzly on the snoot. He'll just come back hungrier."

He set aside the literature and hopped down from the chair. "I'm in the plant rooms and can't be disturbed."

"Not for another twenty minutes. He knows Wolfe's routine as well as you."

"A man's home is his castle, confound it!"

"That's the thing about castles. Somebody's always storming them. Look, we're not working on anything right now. He can't bust us for conducting a private investigation without a license, which is his only beef with us. Let's just swallow the hemlock and get it over with."

He screwed up his round baby face, but he never got quite to the point of actually bawling. "Very well. Give me a moment to prepare."

I left him while he was slipping Encyclopedia Brown page-ends foremost on a shelf of weighty classics he got as much use out of as a stationary bike. He never read anything but whodunits and the *Vine*, the monthly newsletter of the Empire State Tomato-Breeders' Association.

"Season's greetings, Captain." I opened the front door.

It *was* that time of year, but no one at headquarters would dare tell him.

Stoddard shoved past me and into the office, sneered at the framed label from a can of Chef Boyardee, the big globe that still maintained there was a Soviet Union, and the day's display on Lyon's desk, a dwarf tomato plant with fruit the size of buckshot. The boss flattered himself he'd developed a new subspecies, the way Wolfe is doing all the time with orchids, but it was just an undernourished specimen of cherry tomato. His idol's botanical interests are exacting and difficult, but tomatoes practically grow themselves, giving Lyon plenty of time to goof off and read *The Hot-Cha-Cha Murder Case* during his daily four hours total on the roof.

I'll give him this much; the tyrannical cop made him as nervous as he did me, which given my arrest record is no mere qualm, but unless you were sharp enough to catch the slight tremor in his pudgy hands gripping the edge of his desk, you wouldn't know it. He even managed to dial down his frightened treble to a decibel below a dog whistle.

"What can I do for you, Mr. Stoddard?"

The captain, of course, never missed a sign of weakness in others, but for once kept the sadistic note from his snarling baritone.

"Normally I'd say come clean and confess to violation of the New York State Code prohibiting snooping without a ticket on file in Albany, but I'll leave them to another time. You're coming with me to Manhattan."

Sickly green crept into Lyon's cheeks, turning them from McIntosh into Granny Smiths. But he kept his even high pitch. "Out of the question. As you know, I never leave my house on business."

If anything, when our guest smiled he was even more unnerving. "Who said it was business? Never mind. It is."

Without waiting for an invitation, which was customary to him, he plunked himself into the pinkish-orange leather chair facing the desk; it was supposed to be red, like its model across the river, but the upholsterer was colorblind.

"It's my niece," he said. "My brother's daughter."

For once I was more suspicious of him than he was of us. The thought that there should be two Stoddards in existence, and that one of them had procreated, was about as easy to swallow as a tomato-butter sandwich, one of my esteemed employer's more notorious failures.

"Stella's a smart cookie," he went on. "She talked herself into a job in a successful bookstore when she was sixteen, and she's worked there four years. Now her boss suspects her of stealing two hundred dollars from the desk in his office during a Christmas party at the store. I wouldn't be any kind of cop if I thought anybody was above suspicion, but Stella's got too much going on upstairs to risk her job and her freedom over a couple of hundred bucks."

"You are, as you say, a police officer," Lyon said.

"You know damn well I'm a captain."

"As you say." His tone wavered between a high tremolo and a vacuum cleaner. "Why not investigate the case yourself?"

"It's a mystery bookshop. I don't read the things myself; last thing I want to think about when I get home is work, and from what I hear most of them bollix up the facts, putting silencers on revolvers and such. You gobble the things up like candy, so I thought you could shed some light on the nature of the business. The money came from a customer who bought a rare book, in jacket. The owner says that's important. Me, I throw 'em away as soon as I bring home a book."

"Amazing."

Stoddard's normal congestion deepened a shade; but he couldn't tell any more than I could if the chubby little sparrow was referring to the habit or the thought of the captain bringing a book into his house. I figured it was *1,000 Ways to Beat a Suspect to Death*.

"It's got a foreign title." He dug out a fold of ruled paper and squinted at his ballpoint scrawl. "*Fer-de-Lance*, first edition."

Lyon squeaked.

"Thought you'd be interested. Penzler says it was the first book about your god."

"*Otto* Penzler?"

"You know him?"

"We've never met, but I've ordered some items from his shop, and we've spoken on the telephone." Lyon, plainly hooked (he even forgot to be afraid of his company), shook his head. "Something's amiss. Two hundred is far too little for a first edition of that book, which began the Nero Wolfe series, and Mr. Penzler is far too well-versed in his trade to let it go for pennies."

The captain looked again at his notes, rubbed his nose. "Okay, I misread my own chicken scratches. It's a first *movie* edition, with pictures of the actors on the cover and stills from the film inside. That help?"

Lyon nodded, folding his hands across his middle. The fingers just met.

"*Meet Nero Wolfe*, starring Edward Arnold and Lionel Stander. They changed the book's title at the time of release, and almost everything else inside. I have a fair copy myself, but, dear me, I never paid anything approaching two hundred dollars for it. The first, of course, would be worth thousands."

"So somebody got suckered."

"Doubtful. Penzler's reputation is spotless."

"Anyway, he swears Stella was the only one who went into his office between the time he locked the money in the drawer and he discovered it was missing; she'd gone there on some errand or other. What's got me buffaloed is how whoever did it managed to unlock the drawer, take the money, and relock it afterward. Penzler claims to have the only key, and it was on his person the entire time. Stella's good at a lot of things, but second-story work isn't one of them."

I figured if Stella lived up to half the hype she was adopted.

Lyon actually clapped his hands. "A locked-room mystery!"

"It was a drawer, not a room."

"One takes things as they come."

I leaned across the desk and whispered in his face.

"It's a trap. He'll find some way to make you accept payment, and then he'll have you on that practicing-without-a-license rap."

"Fortunately, I'm independently wealthy, and never need to." He raised his voice. "Arnie, we're going to the big island."

I screwed up my nose. "'Book 'em, Danno.'"

Well, the mountain came to Muhammad, the continents drifted apart, and twenty minutes later Lyon finished prying himself into a bilious green overcoat and a Tyrolean hat with a green feather in the band. (Wolfe prefers yellow; the little blob of cholesterol was bound to have an independent streak somewhere.) I'd swear he'd kept the coat unused since before I came under his roof, if I didn't know for a fact he kept contributing to his girth like Methuselah kept having birthdays, and the damn thing fit.

Sitting next to the captain in the front seat of his unmarked Winston Leviathan, Lyon kicking his feet in back, I watched the man behind the wheel scowling at all the decorated windows and bundled-up pedestrians lugging bright packages past decorated windows: He was by Scrooge out of the Grinch by way of the ACLU.

The store was in Tribeca. A hand-lettered sign in red and green announced that the shop was closed for a Christmas party. A burly young employee with a beard buzzed us into a big hollowed-out, well-lit cube walled with books starting at the floor and reaching fifteen feet to the ceiling, with rolling ladders attached to metal rails. Green, red, gold, and silver streamers festooned the place and there was a punch bowl the size of a witch's cauldron and the usual scattering of bottles, partially filled glasses, and abandoned soda-pop cans, along with trays of cookies shaped like Santas and snowmen and Christmas trees that looked like air fresheners, the requisite bowls of untouched nuts, and a basket half-filled with poppy seed buns. A trimmed tree lorded over all in glorious bad taste, in tune with the season.

"Mr. Lyon?" greeted a compact man in an argyle sweater and slacks, wearing gold-rimmed glasses, white hair neatly brushed back, and a snowy, well-trimmed beard. I don't know what I'd expected—a character in a ragged sweatshirt who smelled like old magazines, maybe. All I know about books is the odds at Pimlico. This guy resembled the German scientist who's always explaining Godzilla. "By golly, you look like Archie Goodwin washed Wolfe in hot water and threw him in the dryer with the setting on Normal."

"Mr. Penzler, I presume." Lyon's response was cool, and he ignored the proprietor's outstretched hand; I knew him well enough to know he wasn't offended by the comparison, only to the way it was put. "What is this I am told about someone paying two hundred dollars for a movie edition of *Fer-de-Lance*?"

"It's ridiculous, I agree; but as a collector you must know that when a true first edition prices itself out of most people's market, they turn to the next one down, and yet the next, increasing the value of each in its own order. When I opened this shop, I couldn't give away movie tie-ins; ten years ago, I'd have been lucky to get twenty dollars for one in fine condition. As it was, I made this buyer a bargain, seeing as how he's a loyal, long-time customer; I should add that it was inscribed by Lionel Stander, when he was appearing on *Hart to Hart*."

Lyon asked the customer's name.

"I'm sorry, but that's confidential."

"At least he's intelligent enough not to show himself a gull to the world. Have you another copy? I'd like to refresh my memory."

Penzler scaled a ladder without hesitating and came back with his prize. He'd committed his stock to memory.

"This is a fair copy, with a closed tear in the jacket and a library stamp on the first page. Would you believe I expect to get sixty for it?"

I looked at it over the boss's suety shoulder. A black-and-white photo of a fat, distinguished-looking party and a taller, younger man with a face like a shaved gorilla's, decorated the cover.

Lyon tried to say, "Pfui!" Fortunately for the jacket, it was sealed in plastic; the amount of spraying involved, and the attempt to avoid it, distorted the exclamation so much even Nero Wolfe couldn't have sued him successfully for copyright infringement. He wiped the book on his sleeve. "It's no wonder Rex Stout, acting on Wolfe's behalf, refused to allow any films to be made after the first two-picture contract ended. Edward Arnold was an acceptable Wolfe, but Lionel Stander bore as much resemblance to Archie Goodwin as—"

"Woodbine," Stoddard finished. "Give him the rest, Penzler, just as you gave it to me."

The bookstore owner explained that Stella, the captain's niece, had placed herself in voluntary police custody after the theft was discovered. Penzler had closed the shop early for the party, and as he was too busy to deposit the $200 cash he'd just gotten for the book and reluctant to deprive any of his hard-working employees of party time by making them run the errand, he'd simply locked it in the top drawer of his desk. An hour or so later, he sent Stella into the office to bring back more refreshments. As the celebration was winding down, he returned to put the money in his wallet so it wouldn't be left unattended overnight, and that was when he discovered it was missing.

Lyon asked if she was searched.

"NYPD searched the entire staff," Stoddard said. "The money wasn't on any of them; but anyone could have stashed it anywhere. I've asked the locals to toss the place, but with all these books to look through it'll take days."

"May I see the scene of the crime?"

Penzler smiled. "In all the years I've collected, sold, and written about mystery fiction, that's the first time I've ever actually heard anyone use that phrase."

In the office, our host produced a key and unlocked the top drawer of a graceful-looking antique desk. Inside was the usual desk stuff. "It was on top of that pad: four fifties folded and loose. Don't bother searching the drawer. I've had everything out of it several times."

Lyon pointed at a scattering of tiny brownish-black fragments. "Were those here when you put in the cash?"

Penzler frowned. "I can't say I noticed them."

I had a brainstorm. When you've been a crook all your life, it's not hard to think like a detective. I licked a finger, touched it to one of the fragments, and put it on my tongue. "Poppy seeds," I said. "Not very tasty ones. I saw a bowl of them in the shop. Whoever broke into the drawer must have been eating one at the time."

"Ha!" I know in print it looks like ordinary laughter, but what came out of Captain Stoddard's mouth bore no resemblance to human mirth. "That proves she's innocent. Stella's allergic to gluten. She'd no sooner eat a poppy seed bun than gobble down poison."

Penzler cleared his throat embarrassedly. "I knew that, Captain. It's why I bought them from the gluten-free section of the bakery."

What came out of the cop's mouth next wouldn't read like laughter even in print.

Penzler said, "I don't intend to press charges, or even dismiss Stella; this is the season for forgiving, after all. However, I do think I'm entitled to reimbursement."

"Meanwhile my niece's reputation is destroyed."

Lyon stuck a finger in his ear and commenced to rotate. When it was his right ear, he was just after wax, but when it was his left, as now, he was stroking an idea to the surface of his brain, like a needle coaxing a splinter out of his thumb. So far it had never failed to amount to something just as satisfying. He asked Penzler if he had a magnifying glass.

"I thought all you amateur dicks carried one," Stoddard barked.

Penzler opened another drawer and drew out a square lens in a black plastic frame with a handle. For some time, Lyon studied the inside of the drawer, then dropped to the floor.

I knew it, I thought. The short fat nothing had blown an artery at last; all those greasy gefilte fish his chef, Gus, shoveled into him had taken their ichthyological revenge. But as I was stooping to test his tonnage and calculate the ability of my back to support it, he began crawling across the carpet on his knees and elbows, holding the glass in one hand. It was more physical activity than I'd seen him engaged in ever; the sawed-off porker went begging for a coronary just pushing the button to his private elevator.

He applied the glass again when he reached the paneled wall behind the desk. While the rest of us goggled—Penzler with bemusement, Stoddard with rawboned contempt, and me wondering if I should give notice or just walk out in search of someone to work for who had a couple less bats in his belfry (provided he didn't keep too weather an eye on the business accounts), he crept along like an obese inchworm, training the lens along the baseboard. At length he indicated triumph (I'd worked for him long enough to interpret all his chirps, squeals, and yelps the way a zoologist learns the language of monkeys), flattened himself on the floor, made a rooting motion I couldn't identify because of the fat obstacle he made, and with a noise like a rusty hinge pushed himself back onto his knees and rested his buttocks on his heels, holding up some colored strands between thumb and forefinger. If he could grow a tomato as red as his face at that moment, he'd be Mr. December in the *Vine*.

"Mr. Stoddard, I think the experts in your laboratory will find little difficulty tracing these samples back to the United States Treasury."

"Treasury!" We all said it at once.

"I could be wrong. The new bills are so more colorful than the old that I may be mistaking Christmas confetti for currency. However, I doubt it. Your culprit is a female, hair brownish gray, weighing a few grams at most, measuring perhaps two and one-half inches from nose to tail, and she has accomplices. A mate, for one, and what is doubtless a squirming brood." He thumped the baseboard, calling our attention to a hole the size of a half-dollar.

"A mouse!" Stoddard's tone was disbelieving, but then he'd have demanded a paternity test in the manger in Bethlehem.

"You mean she's shredded my money to build a nest for her young?" Penzler's tone was wounded; even someone as esoteric (I'm pretty sure of the word; I Googled it) as a bookseller is still a merchant, and a dollar destroyed is a heart broken.

"I lost the jacket off a nice copy of Graham Greene's *Brighton Rock* to a rodent with a family, cutting the book to a fraction of its value. New York is an old city, and no matter how many times it rebuilds itself or how clean the neighborhood and its residents, the creatures' bloodlines stretch back to Peter Stuyvesant."

"I didn't know the little bastards could pick locks," I said.

"The Greene was in a chest of drawers, and although it wasn't locked, all they need is a gap in the joints the size of a pencil to gain access. The chest wasn't nearly as old as this fine desk, but time is patient. It will unfasten what is fast and loosen what is snug, no matter how long it takes."

Penzler strode over, helped him grunting to his feet, and stared at the shredded remains of four half-century plants. He gave them to Stoddard, who produced a glassine bag from an overcoat pocket and sealed them inside. "I'll send forensics to scoop out the rest. If you're lucky, Penzler, you may wind up with enough for Treasury to replace the pieces with whole bills."

A weight even heavier than Lyon's seemed to lift itself from the shoulders of the bookseller, who apologized to the captain. "Stella has a raise and a bonus coming, and a public apology in front of the staff."

"Just be sure of yourself next time. Locked rooms and locked drawers. Pfui!"

Lyon was still sputtering at Stoddard's correct pronunciation of the word when Otto Penzler opened the glazed door of a bookcase that matched the desk and handed him something: A book, its jacket sealed in stiff plastic, with a frightened-looking adolescent girl painted on the cover and the title *Secret of the Old Clock*.

"Ha!" Stoddard bellowed again, nastier than before. "Claudius Lyon, I arrest you for practicing investigation without a license, for profit." The ungrateful SOB took a pair of handcuffs from another pocket.

"*Told* you it was a trap!" I said.

I expected another high-pitched noise from Lyon, or at least pallor. Instead, he held the book out to the arresting officer. "You'll need evidence."

Stoddard snatched it from his hand as if he thought he was getting ready to throw the evidence out a window.

"Please examine the flyleaf."

Grinding his teeth, the captain snapped open the cover. Instead of Lyon's, it was his face that faded to a mild shade of mauve. Craning my neck to see past his shoulder, I recognized the leafy tomato plant printed on the bookplate:

Ex libris
Claudius Lyon
700 Avenue J
Flatbush, NY

"In addition to being a bookseller and a scholar, Mr. Penzler operates a number of small presses, one of which produces facsimile copies of great mystery first editions, which he offers at popular prices. When he called to say he'd heard I possessed a first of the inaugural Nancy Drew mystery and asking to borrow it so he could reproduce it, I sent it over by special messenger."

"It came out beautifully," Penzler said. "You'll receive a copy of the first one off the press, inscribed by the publisher. It's the least I can do, since you wouldn't accept remuneration."

"I'll buy it. I wouldn't want to risk Mr. Stoddard's disapproval."

The captain thrust the book back into Lyon's hands and stamped out, leaving us without our ride. Penzler lifted the telephone receiver off his desk and called for a taxi.

I said, "Wait a minute. What about the poppy seeds?"

Claudius Lyon blinked at me. "Not seeds," he said. "Mouse droppings."

I had our cab stop at a drugstore on the way back and gargled with Listerine all the way home.

WOLFE IN CHIC CLOTHING

*"An orderly man is twice as likely as a slovenly one
to make a catastrophic mistake."*

I saw it coming the minute the little boob took *Too Many Cooks* down from the shelf. I just didn't know what lunatic form it would take this time.

He kept all his first-edition Nero Wolfes, bound for him in green cloth—his favorite color—within easy reach because he never made a move without consulting the Gospel According to Archie Goodwin. He'd cracked that nut 10,000 times, but always managed to pick out something fresh to nibble on.

If you're familiar with the series, you know Wolfe is a fat eccentric genius who solves baffling mysteries (usually of the murder sort) when he isn't busy growing orchids or eating ritzy food prepared by his chef, Fritz Brenner. Claudius Lyon—who wasn't born with that name, but picked it up because it's Nero Wolfe inside-out, more or less—is just as fat, and eccentric enough for both of them, but as to genius; well, there's a fine line between it and goofy. He's also a good foot shorter, a fact he failed to consider when he bought his Wolfe-ish townhouse in Brooklyn and filled it with furniture built to his idol's scale. As a result, the big green leather chair behind the Uruguayan fruitwood desk swallows him up when he sits in it and his teeny feet swing six inches short of the floor.

Nevertheless he sits in it four hours every weekday, two of them in the morning and two in the late afternoon, because that's what Wolfe does. The rest of the day he spends with his tomatoes in the plant room on the roof and feeding his fat face with brisket and gefilte cooked by Gus, who is reputed to be the finest kosher chef in the five boroughs; reputed by Gus, anyway. I can barely stomach the stuff myself, and sometimes have to cut and run to Bubba's House of Pork for a break, but it's better than what they feed you in Sing Sing, and it's part of my salary.

Lyon isn't nearly as busy a detective as Wolfe, which is swell by me on account of the royalties he gets from an invention of his dead father's pays the bills. He doesn't charge for his services anyway.

He can't, without a private investigator's license and with Captain Stoddard champing at the bit to bust him the minute a dollar appears in his chubby little fist for a feat of detection. Stoddard's the meanest man in the Brooklyn branch of the NYPD, which is an institution that never recruited anyone on the basis of genteel good manners.

Me, I'm only here because my name is Arnie Woodbine. I type ten errors a minute and the best deduction I ever made put me in the joint for the second time, but when you say the name fast it sounds kind of like Archie Goodwin, who takes notes and does the heavy lifting for Wolfe and writes about his boss's exploits for suety little bookworms like Lyon to read.

Too Many Cooks takes the fat Manhattan genius on a rare train trip to a chefs' convention, which of course leads to murder or Goodwin wouldn't have bothered to publish the account. Wolfe never leaves his brownstone on business, but will do so for recreation, especially if it has anything to do with orchids or the opportunity to increase his belt size.

This time the story gave Lyon the bright idea that he needed to do the same. How could anyone take his loony masquerade seriously if he didn't do everything his role model did, straight down the line?

Don't let anyone tell you being cuckoo doesn't have a rationale of its own.

The catch—one of several—was growing orchids is beyond his abilities, and there are no tomato-growing shows because they could be as boring as his shift in the plant room, which he uses to sneak a few chapters of Trixie Belden and the Bobbsey Twins. Any schmo with the IQ of a TV weather girl can turn a tomato seed into a tomato; it'll do it all by itself if you let it alone. As for preparing food for dining, Lyon can't make a sandwich. Those things stumped him for a while. He sat dandling his sausage-shaped legs under the big desk, pouting like an overfed baby making up its mind where to throw its bowl of strained kale. Which bothered me, because without a client or a whodunit to distract him I couldn't risk adding a zero to my paycheck with him there in the room.

This went on for an hour after he put down the book. I went out for the mail, and when I came back with his copies of *Ellery Queen's Mystery Magazine* and *Shoots & Sprouts* ("Ketchup vs. Catsup: The Controversy Escalates"), I found him foraging deep in one ear with a chunky forefinger. That gesture was his version of Wolfe pushing his lips in and out to indicate he was close to untying a knotty problem after much deliberation.

"Arnie," he said, fastidiously wiping his finger with a green silk handkerchief, "where do you stand in regard to the opera?"

"A block away. Farther if I'm driving." Actually I can take the music or leave it, galloping hippos and all, but I got pinched once sneaking a cashmere coat out of the cloakroom at the Met, and my mug was taped to every ticket booth in town. "Why do you ask?" I pictured him snagging a hat with horns and pigtails and waddling into the chorus.

"I've never given it much consideration myself. Goodwin hardly ever mentions the subject, so I must infer it presents no diversion to his employer." Yeah, he talks like that. I went online so many times to translate what he was saying, the Internet stopped taking my calls. "However, one adjusts as necessary."

I made my face discreet. He encouraged me to needle him, like you-know-who does you-know-who, but rubbing it in about his hopeless battles with botany and vittles would be doing the polka on thin ice. His pudgy kisser screwed tight and turned purple when he got sore; no sight to take to lunch.

"I'll see what's playing." I sat down at my desk and turned on the monitor.

"That would be placing the conveyance in reverse order with the equine. Call my tailor."

"You have a tailor?" He dresses good, give or take an untucked shirttail, in three-piece suits and a tie, after His Portliness, but I assumed he did all his shopping in the Cherubs' section at Skinnerman's. At the time of this narrative I hadn't been with him long enough for him to split his britches and require a replacement.

"Certainly. I'm not a cowpuncher. Krekor Messassarian, spelled the way it sounds. He's in the Brooklyn directory."

Again to spare me the spectacle of that angry-Gerber face I refrained from pointing out that the Yellow Pages is a dandy place to look up somebody from 1993, and opened it. Messassarian wasn't as hard to find as I'd thought; I slid my finger down the *M* column under Clothing and Alterations until I came to a name that ran smack into the margin.

I got him right away. The heavily accented voice walked me through the pronunciation of his name and agreed to come by that evening for dinner and a first fitting.

He turned out to be an Armenian of seventy or a hundred, with bloodhound features and spectacles as thick as glass ashtrays. The badge of his profession, a length of yellow tape measure, hung around his neck. He smelled like a canvas drop cloth that had been left out on the back porch for a year. Messassarian takes too long to write, so I'll just call him Musty.

His head bent close to his blintz to see what he was eating. I couldn't imagine how he handled a bitty thing like a needle. Lyon said he wanted a full-dress suit with all the trimmings: white tie, silk hat, and cape with a white satin lining. If the opera scheme didn't pan out he could always put on the getup and argue Home Rule for Ireland with Queen Victoria. In the front room I helped out by taking Musty's dog-eared memorandum book while he measured, and recorded the dimensions, which were fantastic. The circumference was the same as the height and the inseam was my collar size. A few dozen more bagels with a schmear and a case of cream sodas and Lyon could attend a fancy-dress party as Mr. Potato Head.

The old tailor made miserable noises as he went about his business. I guessed it was all the kneeling and squatting and stooping and squinting at numbers, or maybe it was his way of humming on the job; but Lyon, who knew him better, noticed it too, and inquired about his health.

"Fit as fiddles," the other assured him, and that seemed to end the conversation on the subject. Then he stopped in the middle of measuring for armholes and said, "I am robbed."

Lyon started, chins quivering. "I was under the impression my account was up to date."

"Oh, not by you, Mr. Clod." I swear that's what he called him. I don't doctor these reports the way I do the books. "Someone in my own shop is the culprit. He—or she—has made off with the rarest coin in my collection."

That put the kibosh on that fitting. *Aida* and tomatoes and even the fancy dining, look out! When a mystery reared its big black question-mark-shaped head, everything else was window dressing. As I said, I'm not convinced science would thank Lyon for willing his brain to it, but the only time he didn't seem like just a cheap knockoff was when he had a Gordian knot to sink his fat little fingers into. We adjourned to the office, where Musty sat in the big orange leather chair reserved for the guinea pig of the week while his host squirmed happily on the other side, gulping fizzy cream and burping a merry little tune.

The Armenian, we found out, liked to fool around with obsolete hard currency when he wasn't cutting out suits. He had, he flattered himself, one of the best collections in three counties, exhibited at shows, and two years ago had been named to the Numismatists Hall of Fame by *Jingle*, the magazine of the trade.

"I must confess," he confessed, with another little groan, "to carelessness on occasion. Many is the time I've neglected to return a coin to its case after taking it out for examination or to show to a colleague, and have panicked upon this discovery until the item resurfaced among a jumble of lesser coins on my work table, or in the wrong case due to my affliction." He tapped one of the portable aquariums he saw through. "I can do little about myopia, but I am struggling to eliminate my cavalier tendencies."

"Phooey." Try as he had, the little poseur had never been able to duplicate the Master's *pfui*; each attempt peppered his blotter with spit, so he'd given it up as unsightly and unsanitary. "An orderly man is twice as likely as a slovenly one to make a catastrophic mistake. Overcompensation is the culprit. Please continue."

The coin that had gone astray this time was a doozy: the only known surviving shekel minted in the first century B.C. by one Axolotl II—the Great, was the moniker historians had hung on him. He was a Persian king who had ordered it to be issued to commemorate some great victory or other over a province in China.

"In gold, natch," I interjected, and bent over the PalmPilot I was recording the proceedings in to avoid the peeved-infant look I got from Lyon.

"Zinc, actually." Musty kept his gaze on Lyon. "The material is not so important as the historical value. A most unusual design, no larger than a nickel, but pierced above and below and to each side of Axolotl's embossed profile, representing the four directions of the compass: to the east, the wisdom of the Orient; to the north, the ferocity of the barbarian hordes; to the west, the might of imperial Rome; and to the south, the culture of ancient Greece. Legend says the king was going blind, and decreed the coin contain these tactile features that he might still appreciate its significance by touch. From this you may gather the reason for my interest." Again he indicated his thick cheaters.

"Splendid. Our treasury is more concerned with befuddling potential counterfeiters than celebrating man's accomplishments."

"What's this doodad worth?" I asked.

"Thousands. It's the biggest investment I ever made."

I placed a pensive emoticon beside this transcription. I had as good a chance of laying hands on this piece of Persian plunder as anyone, and I knew a fence who dealt in coins.

Musty groaned again. "It is the old story. When I saw the case was empty, I naturally assumed I'd blundered again and that it would resurface. I'd had it out recently while updating the catalog, so that appeared probable. Yet a number of thorough searches of the shop have failed to turn it up."

"Have you consulted the police?" Lyon's reedy tenor always climbs to a squeak when he refers to the authorities. They represent Captain Stoddard in his mind, and he's even more afraid of that particular paid-up member of the barbarian hordes than I am; and I'm the expert on life in the cooler.

"I am torn as to whether I should. My people have been with me a long time, and I should not wish to subject them to the humiliation of questioning."

I made a mental note (not an electronic one) to remember Krekor Messassarian. If my billet with Lyon ever blew up, I couldn't think of a better sheep to fleece.

Lyon excavated his diamond-and-platinum watch from its vest pocket and folds of fat; the best dip in the state could lose fingers trying to lift it if the pigeon moved wrong. I'd had my eye on it myself, but doubted I could fool him with a tin ringer. Anyway, he was a chicken you could pluck from here to Easy Street if you avoided flash.

"It's late, and I have a morning appointment to show a prime specimen of eastern plum to an official with the Knickerbocker Tomato Council, which may name the species in my honor." This was news to me, and therefore a bald-faced lie, as I was in charge of all communications into and out of the townhouse. Never underestimate the capacity of a little round speck in the firmament to pump himself up into a prize ass. "Please provide Mr. Woodbine with the particulars, including the names of all the members of your staff, and he will conduct a discreet inquiry in the morning."

He hopped down from his chair and circled the desk to offer a puffy little hand. This was the supreme tribute, as in imitation of his personal deity he seldom made physical contact with others of his genus. Musty's reaction was transparent and unappreciative; it was like kneading dough. Lyon entered his private elevator, whose gears hawked and spat and started pulling him up hand over hand to his bedroom.

I spent a quarter-hour wheedling the names and known history of the people who worked for him out of the sap—the old tailor, I mean; it doesn't do to tip one's mitt in front of a pumpkin ripe for the thumping—at the end of which he fingered his tape measure, adjusted the bicycle that straddled his nose, and said, "You *will* be discreet? People think tailors are relics nowadays. The men's store at Skinnerman's offers better benefits and doesn't care whether a seam is stitched by hand or fused with glue. I wouldn't know how to replace them if they're offended enough to resign."

"Trust me, Mus—Mr. Messassarian," I said. Hadn't I sold a venture capitalist his own boat, with his bottle of Asti Spumante still chilling in the refrigerator? "They'll think I'm there to tell 'em they won the New York Lottery."

He went out the front door with a puzzled expression on his long, weary face. Sometimes I lay it on as thick as a $50 steak. Lyon is such an easy mark I'm in danger of losing my fine edge. A man needs a challenge if he's going to hold his own on the pro circuit.

❖

Bright and early the next morning I was in the Brooklyn garment district, which looks a lot like the Manhattan original of times gone by, with workers pushing carts of suits, coats, and dresses hanging from rails across the street any old where in the block, and displays of irregulars in front of cut-rate shops and gaggles of colorful characters pretending to chew the fat on the corners while waiting for something to fall off the back of a truck. (I started to look for my cousin Mickey in the group, then remembered he still had six months left on his year-and-a-day.) Very early Runyon. Messassarian & Sons operated out of a walkup with an open flight of stairs with advertisements stenciled on the risers offering alterations and merchandise. From the age of the layout I figured Krekor Messassarian was one of the original sons.

The room took up an entire floor, with bolts of material on pipe racks and a cutting table the size of an indoor swimming pool littered with paper patterns and pieces of fabric and big shears and thousands of straight pins glittering under strong overhead lights. There was a unisex changing booth behind a curtain and a platform in front of a three-way mirror where the customer du jour could stand and keep an eye on what the tailors were doing with his inseam.

"Just routine," Musty said, introducing me to his staff. "For the insurance. Just routine." If I was the one who'd copped the coin I'd have been diving for the fire escape the third time he said it was just routine. They all gave me the fisheye and went about their work while the boss showed me the locked cabinet where he kept his collection with a little shelf built under it for spreading it out and examining it under a strong glass. There were loose coins on the shelf he said were no great shakes, mixed up with needles and other gear that had wandered away from the work area. The cabinet lock was a Taft. I could have picked it with a noodle.

He had a picture of the missing piece. The Persian king was a weak-chinned jasper with a hoop in his ear. He looked like a female impersonator.

I'd Googled him. He'd gone to war with Rome and lost, the northern barbarians had kicked his butt, and he'd managed to get the Chinese province to sue for peace because the emperor was too busy fighting off the Mongols to give him any time. He spent half his life as a hostage held for tribute and choked to death on a fig. The way I saw it, "Axolotl the Adequate" suited him better. But his coin was worth, well, a king's ransom, so he was my favorite historical figure after Willie Sutton.

Messassarian had three people on staff: a nephew named Norman Pears, shaped like his surname, who at middle age looked a little less like a bloodhound than his uncle, but he had thirty years to catch up; Constance Ayers, his bookkeeper, who wouldn't do any harm to an evening gown and a good set of highlights, but whose mannish suit and mousy brown bun took her down to a seven; and Aurelius Gaglan, a master tailor, who was nearly as old as his employer but dressed better, a walking advertisement for the concern in a fawn flannel suit shaped to his narrow frame, with a fine head of black hair with white sidewalls.

Musty had given me the lowdown on them all the night before. He'd hesitated a bit over Miss Ayers, and when I pressed him he'd admitted she had money troubles, something to do with a deadbeat ex-husband who had left her with his old clothes and bills to pay.

"I have no reason to suspect her, however," the old man had added quickly. "She's been with me for years, and her accounts always balance to the penny. If she were tempted, she could have robbed me blind, without risking so blatant a theft."

But I know a little something about temptation and opportunity, so I saved her for dessert. I set up my interrogation in Musty's office, a pebbled-glass cubicle in a corner out of earshot of the others if we kept our voices low. From behind a desk heaped with books of bound fabric samples, I started with Norman Pears.

"I don't care a jot for Uncle Krekor's little bits of metal." He slumped in the visitor's chair with his knees open and his little pot belly nesting between his thighs. "For one thing I'm not into collecting anything, and for another, I'm set to inherit when he shoves off. The business isn't much, but if you're any sort of detective you can tell he's never spent a dime more on it or himself than he had to. A careful man could live comfortably for the rest of his life on what he's put away."

Musty had told me Pears was in his will; he was his only flesh and blood. "Maybe you couldn't wait. Does not collecting anything include debts?"

"You mean is there a shylock or a bookie in my closet? If there is, you'll find him—if you're any sort of detective."

That was the second time around for that dig. I didn't like the creep, but then I don't have much in common with anyone who doesn't have a shylock or a bookie in his closet. What'd he do for fun, rearrange the gabardine and wait for Uncle Krekor to shove off?

"Okey-doke," I said. "Shoo in Mr. Gaglan."

The tailor was a gentleman, which meant he kept his opinion of my fused-not-stitched seams between himself and the expression on his face. This one collected suits, but since he got the material at cost and did his own fittings they weren't really an extravagance. He was a widower who lived in a furnished room and said he made more money working in the shop then he needed. I wanted even more for him to be guilty than Pears based on that. What's need got to do with dough, I ask you?

Miss Ayers couldn't afford to collect anything. She was so high-strung I wanted to marry her myself just so I could have the pleasure of leaving her with my old clothes and bills to pay.

"I'm the most honest person in the world! I'm so honest I think everyone else is honest, too, which is why I'm in this fix."

"What fix is that?"

"Owing more than I can ever make good. I know Mr. Messassarian told you. He has no right to share my personal troubles with a stranger."

"If you're so sore about it, you shouldn't have shared them with him."

She jumped up and left, making a noise like a cat on helium.

❖

"It's her," I told Lyon. "When I sat her down I was giving her the benefit of the doubt, but she managed to talk me into it. If she takes the stand in her defense the judge will tack on twenty years for something they were trying next door."

He was pouting again. Entering the tomato room without knocking, I'd caught him peeking at the ending of *The Haunted Mill* when he should have been fertilizing the yellow Hibernians. "You've already implicated Norman Pears and Aurelius Gaglan. You're no Archie Goodwin."

"I'm glad you admit it. It's the first step to coming clean and saying you're not Nero Wolfe."

"Stop being nonsensical. I'm merely pointing out that you can't make the same dismal case against three people."

"Maybe they're all in it together."

"Preposterous."

"What about *Murder on the Orient Express*? You made me stay home from the dog races to finish that one."

"You're confusing the issue even further, mixing up fiction with reality."

That one caught me in the breadbasket. It was like the setup for every punch line ever written, and all winners. I didn't know which one to pick.

He took off his apron. It said CHEFS DO IT THREE TIMES A DAY. I'd picked it out deliberately: It was the last time he'd made me do his damn shopping. "Office hours approach. When we get there, be good enough to provide me with a complete description of the establishment."

I took the stairs and beat him; the elevator is as reliable as Lyon is a horticulturist. He heard my report, guzzling cream soda and kicking his feet, then looked at the picture Musty had given me of the coin. He put it down and massaged his brain through his ear. Then he told me to get the tailor on the horn. I listened on the extension, entered some names and numbers into my smartphone, and punched in the first before he could give me my marching orders. That annoyed him more than my outracing the elevator, because he hated not being ahead of everyone else no matter what.

There were five, all men, and only one so far as I knew connected with the case, but I'd sooner confess all my sins to the *Brooklyn Tattler* than acknowledge he'd passed me by after all. He spoke to them not quite in order, one of the lines being busy, so he had to try again after consulting with the next name on the list. That got his goat all over again, on account of that kind of thing never happens to Wolfe. The conversations were brief. He hit pay dirt on the fourth, which would have been the third if the party hadn't been yakking with someone else the first time he tried, but by then he was in a better mood and beyond throwing a tantrum over such a trifle.

I scuttled that by using the phone again.

"Who the devil are you calling?"

"The liquor store. We're out of gin and I know how you get when a guest asks for something and you can't give it to him."

"Who said anything about inviting a guest?"

"No one had to. This is the point in the story where the fat detective hauls all the suspects into his office and exposes his gray matter."

"Put the phone down!"

I put it down. I'm an embezzler, not insubordinate.

He bellowed for Gus, who came shuffling in wearing his rusty tailcoat. "Was it something?" he asked.

"How is our supply of spirits?"

"Gin we don't got."

Lyon thanked him and sent him back to the kitchen. "I told you to have this room soundproofed."

"I did. Gus is psychic. All kosher chefs are. I'm surprised you didn't know that." Actually I'd had the paneling removed and any old shoddy blown in and split the difference with the contractor. I changed the subject by asking politely if I could call the liquor store now.

⚜

He waited in the front room working the Minute Mysteries in Gus's collection of *Cooking for Schlemiels* until showtime. It tore him up not being able to make his entrance directly from the elevator like that other tub of lard, but at the last shindig it had gotten stuck worse than usual and the fire department had to be called, so until we found a repairman as old as the installation he wasn't risking any more such embarrassment in front of company.

I put Messassarian, Pears, Gaglan, and Constance Ayers in green chairs and gave the big orange one to a doughy jasper named Homer Sayles, owner of Homer Sayles Home Sales. That mark of distinction puzzled the others, who had been no less surprised to see him at all at that address. Everyone recognized him and greeted him by name.

I was happy on a couple of counts. For once, after that initial confusion, I'd figured out what Lyon had up his sleeve besides flab. It had come out during that last business call, and since Wolfe never did his own dialing, his protégé couldn't break training just to keep me in the dark. The absence of Captain Stoddard contributed to my air of well-being; this one was outside his jurisdiction, so he didn't have an excuse to show up and make us wet ourselves when he yelled about investigating for profit without a license.

Lyon came in carrying the prop tomato plant for his desk, made a little bow like a toy drinking bird, and hopped onto his chair. His can of soda was waiting. He popped the top, filled a Betty Rubble glass, and passed a little wind.

"I've invited Mr. Sayles, who is germane to the matter at hand," he said, fanning the air with his green handkerchief. "You'll remember, Mr. Messassarian, that his was one of the names you mentioned when I called to ask about the customers who came to pick up their suits the day Axolotl the Great's coin went missing."

The Armenian slid his quadrifocals up and down his long nose, playing miniature trombone. "Yes, but as I told you, all those men are above suspicion."

"Phooey. However, all four of the men you named are, to flatter your gullible turn of phrase, above suspicion in this matter. So are Mr. Pears, Mr. Gaglan, and Miss Ayers. In fact, Mr. Messassarian, you are the only person present who is not."

Musty dropped his teeth. I'm not batting around a cliché. They bounced off the Kazakhstan rug and landed under his chair, where I had to get down on my hands and knees to snare them. After that he sat nervously clacking together the uppers and lowers and extracting from between two incisors a tag I was conscientious enough as cohost of the affair to relieve him of before Lyon saw MADE IN WISCONSIN and stash it in a pocket. The boss, fortunately, was on a roll and disinclined to notice.

"I was inclined at first to suspect Miss Ayers. Of all of you, her finances are the worst, and she became positively hysterical during her interview with Mr. Woodbine. But she is a woman, and therefore given to inexplicable displays of emotion."

The bookkeeper illustrated his point by taking off a shoe and throwing it at him. He squeaked and ducked. Her heel struck Andy Warhol's tomato soup can on the wall behind Lyon's head, cracking the glass in the frame. He wiped his face with his hanky and continued.

"Mr. Pears was my next choice. He stands to inherit, and I'm convinced he has no interest in coins, but he made an unfavorable impression on Mr. Woodbine, whose character judgment is sound. But that was inconclusive."

The roly-poly fraud was making it up as he went along. I'd been arrested twice by policewomen who looked like perfectly respectable hookers. But any sort of character judgment would look uncanny next to his. He'd hired me.

"I had high hopes for Mr. Gaglan. He appears to have no motive and is well-bred, which as we all know predisposes him toward guilt. The culprit is always the least likely suspect. I cite Agatha Christie, Philo Vance, and Mathilda Pearl Worthwhistle for establishing precedent and upholding it. Mrs. Worthwhistle's *The Corpse Blew a Raspberry* is—but I digress. Mr. Gaglan simply defied any connection to the coin's disappearance."

Norman Pears's little pot belly quivered. "So by eliminating everyone else in the shop, you arrived at the conclusion that it has to be Uncle Krekor. What a demented polyp you are."

Lyon did a fine job of imitating Wolfe's immunity to insult, by which I mean he didn't actually bust out crying, just looked like he was about to. I don't know I'd blame him if he did. I've had hemorrhoids I got along with better than Pears, but calling Lyon a demented polyp was hitting it square on the head. A furious clacking from the direction of Messassarian's lap indicated he agreed. He'd dropped his teeth once again.

"You haven't said why Mr. Sayles is here." The Ayers woman had her shoe back on, but the way the broken heel wobbled when she crossed her legs drew a true picture of her sense of composure.

"The reason I asked him to join us is he was fitted by Mr. Messassarian for a tuxedo. The three other customers who claimed their purchases that day were fitted for ordinary business suits."

Aurelius Gaglan had a polite, quizzical smile on his mild face. "I'm afraid I don't understand."

"Mr. Sayles is to be honored by the Brooklyn Real Property Association as its Realtor of the Year. The banquet is not until next week, and since he has faith in his tailor he saw no reason to don it until that evening.

"On the telephone I asked him the same three questions I'd asked the others. One: Have you examined the suit? Two: Have you noticed anything unusual about it? Three: Would you examine it now, purely to satisfy my curiosity? Mr. Sayles was the only man who answered no to question number one, which of course allowed me to skip to number three."

Miss Ayers said, "If you don't start making sense soon, I'll throw the other shoe."

He cringed and stepped on the gas. "This is a picture of the coin. Had I seen it yesterday, this meeting would not have been necessary."

I took the photo from him and handed it to Sayles, whose polite smile broadened when he saw it. He passed it to the woman. She squealed and giggled. Pears snatched it from her, looked, said, "Oh, for hell's sake," and gave it to his uncle. Musty put his teeth back in, fibers and all, peered through his lenses, shook his head, and gave me the expression of a hound that had lost the scent.

Lyon focused on Homer Sayles. "You brought it as I asked?"

The Realtor of the Year nodded briskly and spoke for the first time. "I gave it to Mr. Woodbine."

I went out and brought it back from the hall closet on its padded hanger. On the boss's instructions I unzipped the vinyl carrier and showed them all the sleek black dinner jacket, with Axolotl's profile stitched in place where the second button belonged.

The tailor fingered it, almost touching it with his nose. He muttered a word that was shorter than his name but had just as many *s*'s in it. I recorded it phonetically on my PalmPilot.

"The presence of four holes revealed little, in description," Lyon said. "Visually, the evidence was suggestive. Mr. Woodbine obtained it from a numismatic website. The modern button, common as it is, was unknown in the time of King Axolotl, or he might have selected a design less associated with everyday haberdashery." He waggled a pudgy finger at his tailor. "To avoid a repetition of the mistake I advise you to make an appointment with your ophthalmologist for a new eyeglass prescription, and take steps to reorganize and separate your vocation from your avocation."

⚜

"Splendid. Archie, write Mr. Messassarian a check. Include a bonus of five percent."

I guess when he saw himself in the mirror all decked out in cutaway, cloak, and top hat, Lyon saw Fred Astaire looking back. I saw the little man on the Monopoly box, only fatter.

"For you, no charge," the Armenian said. "You have saved me a fortune and restored my faith in the integrity of my staff."

"I cannot accept. That would constitute payment for my investigative services and bring down the wrath of Mr. Stoddard." He shivered a little.

As for me, I blew my nest egg when Persian Boy ran dead last at Belmont. So I was still working for Claudius Lyon and had to hide my face from security when we saw *Carmen* at the Met.

WOLFE IN THE MANGER

"It's harder to delude yourself into thinking you're the world's greatest fat detective when you're working out of a Motel 6."

"Nero Wolfe?"

"You kidding?"

"Archie Goodwin?"

"That's me."

"It says either one. Sign here." The messenger in the dun-colored uniform stuck out his gizmo and I made a squiggly line on it no graphologist could trace; I knew, because I'd studied the art of forgery before I gave it up on account of all the paperwork. I took what he'd brought and shut the door before he could rethink things.

Who can explain a split-second decision? Automatically accepting offered objects is hardwired into polite Americans. Also, larceny and imposture are part of my DNA. If you don't want a dog to be a dog, don't stick a lamb chop under its snout.

Should the next uniform at Claudius Lyon's door be blue, I could always say I'd misheard the name. Arnie Woodbine sounds a little like Archie Goodwin, if you mumble. Shucks, it's why I was hired. Everything in that Brooklyn townhouse is a Bizarro version of Nero Wolfe's brownstone in Manhattan, from the owner's name to Gus, the kosher chef who can do as many things with borscht as Fritz, Wolfe's man, can do with vichyssoise—except make it palatable to the 90 percent of the population that can't stand beets. I fit square in the middle as a kind of demonstrator-model Goodwin, running errands for my fat employer when I'm not chiseling him. (The last part is pure Arnie.)

The package was hefty, wrapped tightly in Tyvek, and might have been a football, if you filled a football with suet and had a reason to send something as athletic as a football either to Wolfe or to Lyon. In response to a sudden burst of butterflies in my stomach I hoisted it to my ear, listening for ticking or the shifting click of a digital clock changing numerals. No timing device, but if it was a bomb it might have been rigged to explode on opening.

On the other hand, it might be a human head; but I'd been reading too many of Lyon's penny dreadfuls lately, while the local handicappers' sheet was in limbo pending the outcome of a printers' strike. On the other hand, the parcel had been intended for Nero Wolfe, to whom a severed head was a cabbage and nothing more; except even Fritz, his live-in world-class chef, couldn't make coleslaw out of it.

All this diverted me from my natural instinct, which was to keep it for myself, to spend if it was cash or fence if it was jewelry, or hock if it didn't seem too hot. Intended for a big-shot detective like Wolfe, it could have been any of those things as well as something that could detonate. So I raised my loyal chin, placed the bundle on Lyon's desk, and skedaddled to the kitchen to gobble latkes and a bagel while waiting for the boss to come down from the roof, hunching my shoulders against an explosion all the while.

"Was it the doorbell I heard?" asked Gus, shoveling salt into a skillet. "A case, maybe."

He sounded disapproving. Lyon works for free, and is apt to let envelopes from his accountant pile up unopened while he's pretending to detect. I was no longer in charge of the mail since he'd caught me rounding off a check to the next hundred, planning to pocket the difference. He'd have fired me that time if he'd been able to find an Artie Goodman or even a Charlie Dugan in the directory, someone anyway with the right number of syllables and proportion of vowels to consonants to suggest a reasonable facsimile to Archie Goodwin; he's that gone on tracing the original cast.

I shrugged, looking at the *Racing Form* in the rack in front of me for a horse named Surprise Package or some variation. "You've worked here longer than me. How much homeowner's insurance does Lyon carry?"

"Arnie, no."

I looked at Gus and smirked. He'd stopped stirring and turned my way. His long sad face had gone grayer than usual.

"Don't worry, arson's not my line. Anyway, those company investigators put every check endorsement under a lens. A backward kid might be able to match Lyon's scribble, but I'm too sophisticated to pull it off. I just wanted to know if he'd get enough to rebuild the place if anything happened to it. It's harder to delude yourself into thinking you're the world's greatest fat detective when you're working out of a Motel 6. He might just get a bad case of lucidity, and you and I would have to go out and find honest work."

He resumed stirring. "Speak for yourself. I'm a culinary artist."

"The next guy you work for might know the difference between free-range chicken and that pigeon on the ledge you've been overfeeding for months. You can throw all the saffron and sage you want to on it, but it'll still come out of the oven rooting for the old Dodgers. Think there'll be a Christmas bonus this year?"

I'd changed the subject to spare his feelings. We were equal partners in the business of separating Lyon from his finances, but even co-conspirators were capable of sticking their own necks in a noose if they got fed up enough to turn rat. There's honor among thieves; and Santa never misses a yoga lesson.

"Of course there will," he said cheerfully. "People who inherit fortunes never miss a chance to give them away."

"No compunctions about accepting gifts connected with a Christian holiday?"

"He has asked me the same question, phrased more diplomatically. I set his mind at ease. I have many nephews, and the price of bar mitzvah presents, it doesn't go down."

The more he talked about his enormous family the more I was convinced he'd turned up in a basket on the front porch of some temple. I wasn't even sure he was Jewish. The last time his day off fell on Saint Patrick's Day, he'd come home smelling of corned beef and Bushmills.

But who was I to quibble? No one under that roof was what he pretended to be; first and foremost the man who paid the taxes on it.

Speak of the devil. Just then the old building trembled. Either the New Madrid Fault was practicing for the Big One or the elevator was heaving the little slug of lard down from the plant room. I gulped the last of my coffee and hightailed it to the office. Every morning it's important to meet the pig you're carving with a fresh, shiny face.

Lyon came in wearing a green suit—it was his favorite color, but given his abundance of flesh and lack of stature he belonged on a box of Lucky Charms—and carrying a tomato plant in a pot to decorate his desk. Ever since he'd read *Black Orchids* for the umpty-second time he'd been trying to duplicate Nero Wolfe's success with unconventional color breeding, but because tomatoes can be depended upon to turn black all by themselves, with results neither appetizing nor aesthetically pleasing, he was trying for purple. So far all he'd accomplished was a feverish mauve, which tasted like a sunburned potato. He stopped when he saw the package on the blotter.

"Is this a clue?"

Try as he might to sound exasperated—his role model puts up with sleuthing chores only to subsidize his flower-growing, flesh-gobbling, and beer-drinking—he can never quite keep the excitement out of his tone whenever an investigative opportunity comes his way.

"You're the detective," I said. "It was delivered here by mistake. Kype the address."

When he read it he almost dropped the plant. He'd forgotten he was still holding it.

No one ever put down a thing more quickly, not counting a hand grenade, or picked up another thing with more reverence, not counting an ankle bone belonging to an early saint. He tested it for heft. "Who signed for it?"

"He asked if I was Archie Goodwin. I misunderstood, sorry."

"Flummery."

Well, if you're up on his favorite reading, you know where he got that word. If I've given the impression he's dimwitted, I erred. He's just nuts.

"We must see it reaches its intended recipient. Get Wolfe's residence on the phone at once. No, wait."

When he gives an order and he's right there, I carry it out. If you require obedience from your assistant, you can't go wrong hiring a fellow who knows a warm spot when he's found it, especially when he's the shady type. But knowing him and seeing how tightly he was holding on to that package with the magic name on the label, I was pretty sure I wouldn't have to put through that call. It would have been unpleasant, because Wolfe was well aware of this sedulous ape's existence, and deplored it; but it was hero worship that turned the thing in the end. I cradled the receiver on my desk and waited.

"We should examine the contents first," he said. "The man has enemies, and there is such a thing as—"

"Professional courtesy?"

His cheeks, normally as red as an organically grown tomato, lost a little color over the adjective. He is half-convinced that Captain Stoddard of Brooklyn Bunco has the place bugged, hoping to catch just such a slip. Before licensing a private eye, the State of New York requires proof of police experience or tenure with a legitimate detective agency. Lyon has neither. The moment he starts calling himself a pro, which means he's charging for his services, a flying squad will pounce on the building with a warrant for his arrest. Then Stoddard will have it condemned and the site sown with nonkosher salt so nothing will grow in its place.

"Good Samaritanship," Lyon corrected me. "It is the season, after all. Where do you think you're going?"

I was at the door with my hand on the knob. "If you're sold on blowing yourself up on Wolfe's behalf, don't you think there ought to be a survivor to tell him about it?"

"Don't be an ass. Find Sherm David."

Sherm's place in his orbit is an example of Lyon's contortionist brain at its most active. When Goodwin isn't enough, Nero Wolfe always turns to Saul Panzer, the best street snoop on the East Coast. The day Sherm came to the kitchen door asking for a handout, Gus had been set to shove the door in his face, but Lyon happened to be present, supervising a brisket. Curiosity being his only strong trait I consider normal, he'd asked the beggar his name. The Biblical David being Solomon's father, Sherman being the name of an armored vehicle, and *Panzer* being German for "tank"; do I need to beat everything to death?

If I come any closer to understanding the way the man's mind works, mine will cease to work at all.

The Lord looks after lugs and loons. He must, or how could a household made up of a first-class sneak thief, confidence man, and forger, a cook who doctors the accounts as often as he seasons the soup, and a certifiable schizo keep operating with a high-ranking cop circling overhead day and night, watching for a single misstep? Sherm and I don't get along. He smells like Gus's spoiled lox, for one thing, and like any good scoundrel he knows another when he sees one and is always wangling for a scheme to expose me and worm his way into my cozy indoor job; but he'll do almost anything for a buck—anything for a twenty, which is rarer than you might think, cynical as you are.

Anything. Even open a package that might blow him all over Jersey and clear up to Buffalo.

"Find him how?" I had to ask Lyon, as much as the picture of Sherm David being buried in smithereens appealed to me. "His refrigerator box isn't listed."

"Surely the years you've spent in my proximity have had some effect. What's the metaphorical phrase reporters admire so much? 'Police are scouring the city.' Scour."

I boiled at that. Not just because he has it in his curdled mind he's a genius, but also because he is more of a hothouse product than all his tomatoes combined and couldn't find his way to the end of the block, let alone peek under every moth-eaten knitted cap in the borough looking for Sherm's scabby face and hit-and-miss whiskers. I went upstairs, changed into my grubs, and steeled myself for the Cook's tour.

The shelters came up craps, but I caught a break at the second flophouse I tried. A fiver to an androgynous heap of rags camped out on the linoleum in the foyer, waiting for a vacancy, got me directions to a gas station on Flatbush, whose owner rented squatting space in a van parked behind the building for a buck a day: Sherm had left the address with the heap of laundry, who owed him money and had given him an unscratched lottery ticket as collateral. I drove there in the boss's München two-door, a hybrid, snatched open the van's rear doors without knocking, and stepped back, as much to let *eau de Sherm* out into the air as to avoid any self-defensive maneuvers from inside. On his best day he smelled like the alley between a Vietnamese restaurant and a shelter for homeless cats.

The tenant was *hors de combat*, snoring gin fumes into the headliner on a blanket of bedbugs. I'd lugged along a pint of Old Organ Donor from Lyon's cellar (it was Bombay Sapphire in the account book), and brought him around by holding his nose and pouring a dram down his throat when he opened his mouth to breathe.

When he'd finished gagging and throwing windmill punches that didn't connect, I saw recognition in the yellow-orange eyes straddling the potato nose and gave him the lay.

"Twenty-five," he said. The nature of the job didn't seem to faze him. "My rates go up after six."

"It's only half-past noon."

"Which noon?"

"December."

"Meal in it?"

"The condemned always gets one."

"Is it herring? I like Gus's herring."

"Tonight it's blood soup."

"Make it thirty."

"Scratch the lottery ticket. Maybe you lucked out."

"I scratched it. Does this look like the Ritz?"

I nailed a roach with the heel of my hand and rubbed it off on orange shag. "Maybe some curtains, posies in a vase—"

"Thirty."

"Nuts. It's Christmas. You know how much you can clear in that neighborhood in a day with your hat out? And you don't even have to leg it. I got a blanket in the trunk."

"I ain't riding in no trunk."

"I wouldn't ask you to, in respect to the trunk."

"Think it's a bomb?"

"Your troubles are over if it is. Turn down the job, there might not be another. Where you going to find another touch like Claudius Lyon in this life?"

"Where're you?"

I grinned. "That's the spirit. Who knows? This could be the day you crowd me out."

"If this was that day, that ticket would've been good. Gimme that bottle. Explosions aren't always final. I should anesthetize myself, in case I lose an arm or an ear."

⚜

Gus, with his chef's smeller, never lets Sherm inside, so I brought the package out to him on the stoop, carrying it left-handed in case it wasn't powerful enough to leave a crater where I'd been standing. He took it down the block while I waited in the foyer with my fingers in my ears. Five minutes later the doorbell rang and the bum, still in one piece, traded something in loose wrapping for the double sawbuck I'd promised.

I'd been right to compare its weight to suet. When Lyon laid it on his desk and spread the paper, he wrinkled his bulbous baby's forehead over some kind of sausage in a slick white casing, big enough to last him three squares. He leaned down and sniffed.

"Schweidnitzenschnitzel."

"Gesundheit. What's in the package?"

He repeated the word. I had to look up the spelling in his big dictionary before I could Google it; Webster and the Net had nothing to add to his definition: "It's a wurst, made originally in eastern Germany. Extremely pungent and extremely expensive. Gus served it just once, before your time. We haven't been able to find it since." He looked at the return address. "Why, the market's just upstate. Perhaps he ordered it as a surprise."

Summoned, Gus looked at the item and shrugged. Lyon rubbed his hands.

"A mystery. We may as well dine while I work on it. Thick slices." He gave it to Gus. I let him carry it as far as the door before I opened my mouth.

"Hold the salt."

Lyon paused, turned his head as far as it would go my way on what he called a nick. "And why should I do that?"

"It doesn't go with arsenic."

He frowned, but he didn't puzzle long. "Of course. I forgot for a moment to whom it was addressed."

I didn't bother telling him his memory had been fine until he found out the package was edible. I'm supposed to needle him, Goodwin fashion, but I've learned the best way to do that is to refrain from putting it into speech. He was preoccupied, however, and didn't notice. "Arnie. Have it analyzed. Just one slice, in case it turns out to be benign."

Grogan's Pharmacy was the place. Grogan rings up Lyon's Tums and hemorrhoid ointment at three times the price and we split the difference. This one would be the jackpot. Business was slow, and he called after just an hour to report the whatchamacallit had tested negative for toxins. Once again a pair of pudgy hands got rubbed. "Satisfactory. Just in time for supper."

When he finished telling Gus the good news over the house phone, I asked him what all that guff was about sending the package to Wolfe.

"We can't very well do that with a slice missing." He looked at the clock and hopped down from his oversize chair. "Call the market in the morning and order a fresh Schweidnitzenschnitzel to be delivered to him."

He was overlooking something, but I didn't say anything for fear he might say "Schweidnitzenschnitzel" again. I knew he'd get to the something after he'd attended to the important detail of stuffing his face. Like I said, he's as smart as he is screwy.

We'd been sitting in the dining room a couple of minutes when Gus came in carrying a covered tray and wearing a bewildered look. When he set it in front of Lyon and lifted the lid, I saw why. The overgrown wurst was cut into slices less than halfway, and something was poking out the end where he'd stopped. "My knife hit something, I think maybe bone? But no."

Lyon used his own knife and fork to clear the meat away from the foreign object. When he had it free he wiped it off with his napkin and held it up. It was a statuette of a bearded man in a robe and holding a staff with a curved end. It was about seven inches tall and made of something yellow.

"Carved by hand," he said, turning it over in his hands. "No markings. Get me a needle and matches."

I didn't ask, only acted. I figured it would take me long enough to find a needle in an all-male household without the extra delay. Finally I came down from my room and handed him something. "No needles. Will this do? I took it from a new shirt."

"Actually it's better. I won't burn my fingers." He took the pin by its round plastic head, struck a match from a box Gus had brought from the kitchen, and held the flame under the pointed end until the metal glowed red. Shaking out the match, he stuck the point into the statuette's flat base, then got rid of the pin and sniffed at the tiny hole he'd made. "Ivory, as I suspected. Subjected to intense heat it smells like burnt hair."

I filed that tidbit away in case I ever had to go back to second-story work. It might save me from embarrassing myself in front of a fence. "Looks old."

"It is. The workmanship is Byzantine. The image is a shepherd, I'm fairly certain."

"Nativity figure," Gus said. We stared at him. He spread his hands. "What, I can't know this?"

Corned beef, I thought; the old fraud. To Lyon: "Why pick a Christmas knickknack in a salami and ship it to Nero Wolfe?"

"Subterfuge suggests crime. Have you been maintaining the newspaper archive?"

His god keeps back numbers for reference, so of course we must also. "As I keep telling you," I said, "there's a little invention called the computer that does all that for you. I'll check to see if anyone's copped a holiday display this yuletide."

"Do so. And when you call the market, ask who placed the order and who had access to the sausage. Also find the messenger who brought it. That was no error. Someone might confuse me for Wolfe, but no one would mistake Brooklyn for Manhattan."

There it was, the thing I'd thought of before but he hadn't. Told you he'd get around to it. Now that he had, I beat back the urge to laugh in his face for thinking anyone would take him for Wolfe. The doodad he was holding had a better chance of passing itself off as the Statue of Liberty.

❧

I swiveled from the computer. He looked up from *Encyclopedia Brown, Boy Detective*. "St. Cecily's here in town, last week," I said. "When a novitiate came in to sweep up, he was almost trampled by the thief making his getaway. Said thief was interrupted before he could swipe more than one figure from the manger on display. Shepherd, part of a set made in Byzantium in the third century, artist unknown. Where'd you learn about Byzantine craftwork?"

"It featured in Sherlock Holmes. I looked it up."

"Which story?"

"It was a graphic novel."

"You mean a comic book?"

He changed subjects. "Did the novitiate see the culprit?"

He actually uses words like that. "Happened too fast. The whole shebang's estimated upwards of fifty thousand. Nine pieces. Almost five grand for a hunk of elephant molar."

"Less. The infant Jesus would be worth the most, followed in descending order by Mary, then Joseph, then the Wise Men, then the shepherds. Were there camels?"

"Doesn't say."

"I like camels," he said wistfully.

He does. An ugly Day-Glo-on-velvet painting of a desert caravan hangs directly opposite his desk, over the peephole one or the other of us is supposed to spy on so-called confidential conferences in the office—a la you-guessed-it—but there haven't been any so far. At a guess I'd say his interest in camels is a case of sympathizing with a fellow mammalian oddity.

"I dislike thieves of religious antiquities," he said then, without wist. "Leads?"

"Apparently not, but police are scouring the city."

When he scowls he looks like the Gerber kid with gas. "On second thought, don't call the meat market. Go there in person tomorrow. Our shepherd seems to have taken a trip upstate."

⚜

The town, near the Connecticut border, had probably been a Mayberry sort of place before gift shops, antique stores, and Ye Olde pubs had moved into its two-block business section, shoving out the hardwares and corner groceries that give a place its pulse. Mike's Meats stood just off the main drag, a blockhouse relic of earlier times with a cartoon of a fat jolly butcher on the sign, festooned in a string of wieners. The owner turned out to be a skinny Arab with a miserable expression tattooed on his face. I still don't know who Mike is or was.

It was a busy morning, with customers loitering over the ribs and chops in the display cases while waiting for their numbers to be called. When mine came up I opened with an order of Schweidnitzenschnitzel to be delivered to Nero Wolfe's address. The Arab showed no special reaction, so I asked him flat out if any others had been ordered there recently. I put a stubborn look on my face and he left off in mid-sigh to check his records.

"I have nothing," he said afterward, "but one of my people quit last week without giving notice. He may have taken the order and forgotten to put it in the book."

"Absent-minded type, was he?"

"Not really. He was a steady worker. I wish I had more."

"Did he give any reason for quitting?"

"He said he was going on a religious retreat to Jerusalem."

"Was he pulling your leg?"

"If he was, it was the first time. He wasn't a jokester." He quoted me a figure for the sausage that ought to have included an ivory camel inside. I didn't think there was any room there to jack it up for the expense account. I left with the name of the employee, his last known address, and a sour mood.

⚜

"Simeon Poldaski," I reported, when the boss climbed onto his chair, burping wurst. "His landlady said he packed up his things and left the day he quit the market. Told her the same thing about hopping a plane to the Holy Land. I tried all the airlines, but these days they're clammed up tight; wouldn't tell me the time by the clock over their left shoulder."

"Hypothetically I'm inclined to accept our man's explanation. His name suggests a Catholic upbringing. If his conscience is troubled by his theft from a church, sending the evidence to a distinguished detective to rid himself of it and embarking on a pilgrimage to atone for his sin makes excellent sense."

"Why not return it to the place he took it from?"

"Penitents are often in a hurry to obtain absolution. Faced with the alternative of driving to a distant community or drawing the authorities directly to the town from where the package was sent, he settled upon this circuitous plan to give himself time to complete his travel arrangements while avoiding arrest. The airlines are busy this time of year; he might not have gotten a seat right away. Certainly Wolfe would have no trouble making the connection to St. Cecily's, but he hasn't a reputation for involving the police until he's finished his investigation."

"He doesn't work for free."

"Incorrect. He sometimes accepts a challenge merely for spite or out of personal pride. It's not inconceivable that such a profane crime would find him in a seasonal mood. Does Poldaski have a family? He may make contact."

"He's barely on the grid. I dug up a brother, but I know even less about him."

"And I thought all human knowledge was on the Internet."

"So is all human ignorance. Some folks just don't register."

"I still refuse to submit to the coincidental theory. Someone connived to divert that package here. What do you remember of the messenger?"

Goodwin has a crack memory. Mine's just better than average, congenitally speaking, but after I served a stiff stretch for selling hot merchandise to the same undercover cop a second time, I'd trained myself to observe details and hang on to them. "Five-eight, brown eyes, broad face, cold sore on his upper lip."

He pointed at the telephone. "Convey that description to the service. I'll listen on the extension."

Listen is all he'd do. His telephone phobia is the only idiosyncrasy he shares with his nonparticipating mentor that he came by honestly. His voice goes up a full octave when he speaks on it, squeaking like a balloon on the higher notes.

"Mercury Couriers." An icy feminine voice.

I told the voice's owner I was a detective—leaving out the "private" part—and said I needed to locate an employee on a matter of grave importance. She listened to the description, but it rang no bells; it was one of the smaller services, she explained, and she knew all the personnel. I looked to Lyon, who merely shrugged. I was on the point of thanking her anyway and hanging up, when she interrupted.

"Has this anything to do with the attack on Lloyd Berber?"

Cagily, I replied that that was official business I wasn't at liberty to discuss.

What I got, through sly questioning, was this:

Someone had jumped this Berber on his rounds yesterday, knocking him out with a blow from behind, and stripped him of his uniform. He was in Presbyterian Hospital under observation for a possible concussion. A single package was missing from his truck, addressed to—

We hung up after getting the name. Lyon, trying hard not to betray his excitement, opened his desk drawer to count the pull-tabs inside. They belonged to cans of cream soda, his beverage of—well, not exactly choice. The copycat purist in him would prefer beer, but half a bottle is sufficient to send him strolling down Avenue J stark naked; which you don't want to see. Trust me.

When I finally shook that image out of my head, I looked over and saw him rooting around in his ear with a forefinger. He wasn't after wax. He was poking at his brain for the solution that was buried just under the surface.

⚜

Police Captain Stoddard's furious face and balled fists showed up in the foyer twenty minutes later. Normally he's about as welcome as a bleeding ulcer, but Lyon had established a new precedent by having me call him at headquarters and issue an invitation. I'd attended to my bladder in preparation for the visit, but it was still a near thing as I conducted him to the office. Lyon's voice sopranoed more in his presence than when he talked on the phone, but he managed to hand him the name he'd written on a sheet of paper without dropping it.

"Who the hell is Taddeus Poldaski?" Stoddard demanded.

Lyon squeaked, "He is Simeon Poldaski's brother."

"And who the hell—?"

"I—we—suspect Simeon of stealing this item from St. Cecily's Catholic Church last week." Lyon took the shepherd figure from the deep drawer of his desk and stood it on top.

Stoddard seized it in a hairy fist and looked it over top to bottom. "Where'd you get it? How long have you had it? By God, I've been waiting for this. Withholding evidence in a felony investig—"

For the second time in ninety seconds, the fat little guy cut in on Stoddard in midstream. He was pale and his jaw quivered, but I had to hand it to him. I don't know now if I'd have the guts. "With respect, sir, in the little more than twenty-four hours we've had it, we weren't able to determine for certain that it was the property stolen. Indeed, we're still proceeding on the assum—"

This time the captain did the butting in. "I asked you where you got it."

"I shall supply that information after you locate Taddeus Poldaski and bring him here so that Mr. Woodbine can identify him—or not, if that should be the case."

"I can't arrest a man without evidence, and I sure as hell can't arrest him for being the brother of a crook; if he even *is* a crook. And I sure as *hell* wouldn't bring him here. I'd take him to headquarters and sweat a confession out of him."

The cop's face was red, Lyon's dead white. But his vocal cords remained in working order, although they could've done with a drop of oil. "I apologize, Mr. Stoddard; I was unclear. We—I—suspect Simeon Poldaski of the church theft. We're also proceeding on the assumption that Taddeus is responsible for assaulting Lloyd Berber, a messenger with Mercury Couriers, in Manhattan the next day."

"That isn't my jurisdiction."

"Yes. I'm not an expert, but it seems to me that in the spirit of cooperation, once you've closed your neighbors' case, you'll close yours."

They went back and forth. Stoddard threatened to haul us in as material witnesses unless we told him why we thought I could finger Taddeus for Berber, what that had to do with the incident at St. Cecily's, and why we were so damn sure Simeon was behind that;

but Lyon stuck solid as a gob of goo in a drainpipe. It probably cost him the price of a pair of shorts, but he outlasted the purple artery pounding on the side of the captain's neck. He called Lyon a name that would shock a pirate, and blew on out, carrying the ivory piece and slamming every door on the way.

I broke the loud silence. "He took it better than expected."

Lyon mopped his face with a green hanky. "Do you think he'll do as we asked?"

"Sure. No self-respecting cop would pass up the chance to break a case in his own backyard and show up the competition in theirs at the same time. Question is, will he make good on his promise? They don't let you grow tomatoes in Sing Sing."

He picked up Encyclopedia Brown and found the place he'd marked with an old slice of bacon while I played with the germination records software in the computer; but in ten minutes with his nose stuck in the book I never heard him turn a page.

⚜

Next day was Christmas Eve. I got up from *Mr. Magoo's Christmas Carol* to answer the doorbell, reflecting on Magoo's myopia, an affliction Lyon shared, but only in his brain.

Stoddard barged past me into the office. "It was the McCoy. The pastor identified it. Now spill."

Lyon flicked off the TV. "Have you found Taddeus Poldaski?"

Stoddard barked into a cell. A patrolman brought in a shortish character, saluted, left. Taddeus wore a gray suit, cheap but a good fit, with a red tie. It was an improvement over his messenger's uniform. I looked from the cold sore on his lip to Lyon and nodded. The little man behind the big desk squirmed happily in his chair. "You took the messenger's place and delivered a parcel bound for a Manhattan address to this one instead. Why?"

All he got for an answer was a sullen look. Lyon turned up a palm made of pink Play-Doh.

"The question may as well be rhetorical. Your brother, in his repentance, told you of his crime and that he'd sent the evidence to Nero Wolfe. I assume it was a fait accompli, since you failed to stop him. You acted to postpone or prevent an official solution. Was it fraternal love or self-protection?"

Stonewall. Stoddard put in a big flat toe. "You say your brother's in Israel. The State Department might not extradite him just for burglary, but I hear that messenger you conked might not pull through. Accomplice to murder will swing the deal."

"That's impossible. I barely hit him."

Stoddard's jaw clamped. Anyone else's would've dropped open. I knew what he was thinking: *The little toad hit a homer.*

Well, the captain had set it up with that whopper about Berber, whom we'd heard had recovered and been sent home; but even so. Before this, all he'd seen Lyon solve were word games.

Shaken, Taddeus dropped into the orange chair reserved for guests of honor. "I can't let Simeon take all the blame. We both worship at St. Cecily's. He told me he was short on cash, had acted on impulse, and what he'd done then. I panicked. I'm being considered for a federal job. It's not very important, but it requires screening for criminal activity and associations. I'd be sunk if it got out my brother's a felon. It took only a call, pretending I was Simeon, to find out where the messenger was on his route." He breathed in and out. "The rest you know."

"Not quite," Lyon said. "As the only one close to the thief, you were the logical candidate for the second crime. But surely you know, even if you delayed the investigation long enough to be hired, your superiors would have dismissed you the moment the truth came out."

"That's just it. Everyone knows you're a joke, and Woodbine's a crook who'd say he's Cap'n Crunch to get his hands on something that might be valuable. I thought with you two in charge, it was better than throwing the package in the river."

Lyon pulled his baby's scowl. Stoddard's grin looked like a crocodile crossed with a bear trap. He called the patrolman back in and had Taddeus cuffed, Mirandized, and removed.

"St. Cecily says they won't press charges now the dingus is recovered," Stoddard said. "It's that time of year. But the brother's still on the hook for the messenger. Gimme the wrapping the package came in."

I fetched it. He sniffed at it. "Smells like meat."

Lyon told him about the Schweidnitzenschnitzel. "Some courier services x-ray parcels looking for hazardous material. Someone might have recognized the shape and reported it. Simeon found the ideal camouflage right where he worked."

"Gimme this Schweiden-whatsit too. The DA likes to be thorough."

"Unfortunately, so do I." Claudius Lyon stifled a belch.

WOLFE AND WARP

"You can't be Wolfe without a supervillain of your own to fight, so you're studying up on how to build one from scratch."

I was processing the final draft of Claudius Lyon's essay for the *Urban Herb and Vegetable Growers' Bulletin* ("Cherry Tomatoes: Miniature Perfection or Genetic Dwarfism? Part III") when a shadow fell across the keyboard. The little pipsqueak's fulsome prose had my thoughts so tangled I hadn't heard Gus enter the office.

The kosher chef and door-opener of our establishment was holding one of the three-by-five cards he wrote his recipes on, but the way he carried it, by one corner like a dead rat by its tail, suggested it contained something less pleasant than a list of the ingredients of his famous (in that house, anyway) horseradish sauce.

I didn't take it. I'd broken the very American habit of accepting whatever was thrust at me the last time I was served with a warrant. "What's the errand this time, fertilizer? I told him last time I wouldn't take any more of his—"

"Books."

"Whose book? I told Manny the Monk I'd pay him next Tuesday."

"Books. Printed paper with a cover glued on. Mysteries. He wants you to bring 'em back from the liberry."

I won't say my jaw dropped; the last time Arnie Woodbine's jaw did that was at age fourteen, when the judge ruled against trying him as an adult. But bringing mysteries to that particular Brooklyn townhouse would be like delivering seafood to SpongeBob SquarePants.

Lyon had had the walls double-reinforced to support many tons of Lord Peter Wimsey and Basil of Baker Street, but he'd overlooked the foundation, and kept a team of lawyers busy preventing the city building inspector from prowling inside the crumbling basement. He can afford to support those sharks in gray worsted; he's loaded, which is good for him, because his collection is largely worthless. I have that on the authority of the rare-book dealer I tried to sell some volumes I'd snitched off the shelves. He'd read the covers off half and made notes in the rest in his moronic scrawl, and you can't give that stuff away.

I snatched the card from Gus. *Fantômas. The Insidious Dr. Fu Manchu. The Testament of Dr. Mabuse. The Memoirs of Sherlock Holmes.* I brought it within eyelash length: Yep, that's what the hen had scratched.

"I don't know about the others," I said, "but he donated all his Holmes to B'nai B'rith last year: Said he knew it all by heart, but the truth is he's intimidated by Sherlock's brain power. The only reason he picked Nero Wolfe to imitate is they're both fat."

"Can I tell him you'll do it or not? I got a mess of potato latkes in the oven and two more pans waiting to go in. You know once he starts noshing on them I got to get out the coal shovel."

I was plenty sure Archie Goodwin, my opposite number in the Wolfe household, didn't do delivery-boy duty unless it was a suspect or a vital clue; but I'm a thief, and my probationary officer considers unemployment a mark on the red side of my rehabilitation ledger.

"What do you think?" I asked.

He didn't reply except with a smug look. Gus and I had been fleecing the boss for years and had few secrets from each other.

Libraries make me nervous. To duck arrest for picking the pocket of a sports coat hanging on the back of a reader's chair, I'd let security take my picture in the local main branch, and it had been sent to all the others. That meant hiking all the way to the New York Public Library in Manhattan, and a subway ride back with all the other sardines packed in at rush hour, with a load of books under each arm.

I got a break, though, winning a race with a woman in her third trimester for a seat that had just opened. The books gave me an excuse to avoid a lot of angry eyes. I read just enough in each volume to suspect a pattern, and when I lugged the stack into the office just as the big chair behind Lyon's big desk was swallowing him whole, he confirmed the point: He slid the petrified slice of bacon he used for a bookmark—kosher chef Gus would settle for no other use of it—from a copy of *And Be a Villain*.

"I know that one," I said, dumping the pile onto the desk. "That's where Nero Wolfe meets Arnold Zeck."

"It is." Raising the volume, he pretended to lose himself in Rex Stout's prose as dictated by Goodwin.

I picked up each book in turn. "Fantômas. Fu Manchu. Dr. Mabuse. Professor Moriarty. Now Zeck. All criminal masterminds. You went round the bend before we ever met, but now you're on your third lap. You can't be Wolfe without a supervillain of your own to fight, so you're studying up on how to build one from scratch."

"Once again, Arnie, you demonstrate the exact measurement of the abyss that exists between your intellect and mine. Why should I whip up a nemesis when I already have one ready-made?" Without taking his nose from the page, he indicated my desk with a pudgy pink palm.

Across the keyboard of my word processor lay a copy of the *Garden State Gazette*, a tabloid based in Jersey City. Before placing it there, he'd folded away the front-page picture of a swollen-headed space alien seated in the Oval Office to an inside article headed:

FURNITURE KING'S DAUGHTER MARRIES TYCOON'S SON

It was a more-or-less standard society piece covering the wedding of one Daffodil Warp to Hyman Brill III, only child of Hyman Brill Jr., a billionaire venture capitalist living in Newark; but it had a smarmy slant, implying that the union was a merger of fortunes rather than a match made in heaven. The bride's father, one Delmer Warp, had made a fortune selling estate furniture. He'd had the inside track as a longtime mortician, snapping up antiques cheap from bereaved families of his clients and selling them for five times what he'd paid. Five years of that and he'd sold the undertaking business in order to manage his chain of furniture emporia across the state of New Jersey.

"Huh!" I wasn't sure if I disliked Warp based on his face in the wedding photograph, pale and bald, with coarse white hair sprouting from his ears and a nose like the corner of a skyscraper, or because he'd stumbled on a racket I'd overlooked.

"Sooner or later," Lyon said, "we two planets were bound to collide; I saw it the moment I read the article. Anticipating that, I must arm myself with the methods employed against the archfiends in these books."

"Yeah, I get it. Arnold Zeck equals Delmer Warp. You went three letters past *A* and three back from *Z* and got your man, just like Gus mixes cream cheese with lox and spreads it on a bagel. What if Warp don't come near your orbit? Am I supposed to hogtie him and drag him into it?"

"That won't be necessary. I've an appointment with him in this room tomorrow morning."

⚜

It came about like this:

Daffodil Warp (it's a crying shame what parents do to defenseless infants) had come back from her honeymoon in Acapulco, sobbing into Daddy Delmer's vest that bridegroom Brill had disappeared. He'd left the hotel, he'd said, to buy an English newspaper, and had never returned. Having stumbled upon Lyon's advertisement in the Newark *Star-Ledger*:

Vexed? Stymied? Up a tree? Consult Claudius Lyon, the world's greatest amateur detective. No fees charged. Your satisfaction is my reward. Apply in person at 700 Avenue J, Flatbush.

Warp had immediately called for an appointment, apparently while I was out buying tomato seeds from Lyon's favorite gardening shop clear out in Canarsie. There was no mystery in why the little chub worked for free: He's filthy rich, as I said, thanks to an invention of his dead dad's, and the moment Captain Stoddard of Brooklyn Bunco hears he's been paid so much as a Canadian penny for conducting an unlicensed private investigation, we'd be raided. Nor did I have to scratch my head over why Warp would choose the boss over a legitimate dick like Wolfe: Self-made millionaires are notoriously stingy when it comes to coughing up dough for services rendered.

Just how my generous employer intended to turn a high-profile client into a supercriminal was worth postponing an update to my phony resume.

Warp's nose looked even more out of proportion to his thin pasty face through the two-way glass we'd installed in the front door a la Wolfe's, in place of the old peephole; but it was a flat pane, not a fisheye, so the truth was the man went through life looking as if he were staring through both sides of an aquarium. He had Daffodil with him, and if anything she'd inherited the family physical trait in spades, and red to boot, no doubt from bawling; she could have guided Santa's sleigh through a roaring blizzard.

"Welcome!" I said, flinging open the door on a grand or two, if I could just talk Lyon into accepting a retainer despite his fears I knew a lawyer who could help him hide it, if we could stall the client along for two-to-five till he got out; he'd split his fee with me. "I'm Arnie—"

Which is as far as I got before Delmer Warp unburdened himself of his Homburg and camel's-hair coat and bundled them into my arms.

I thought about hurling them into a corner. It's what Goodwin would have done; but he wasn't working for a man who could wind up in a room lined with mattresses and in no further need of an assistant. I hung them up in the hall closet and hotfooted it to beat our guests to the office door. All the townhouses of that vintage were laid out identically, so no detecting skills were required on our visitors' part to find the most likely room for doing business.

I had to admit the expression on the face of the squirt behind the desk was beginning to resemble a scowl and not so much a colicky baby about to throw a tantrum. He'd been practicing in front of a mirror, probably with a picture of Nero Wolfe stuck in the frame for comparison. The pint-size hypocrite was delighted in inverse ratio to the look of annoyance. His idol's reluctance to stir himself to solve a case was legendary, while he himself couldn't wait to show off what he'd learned by reading up on Wolfe's cases.

Not that much sleuthing would be needed to get to the bottom of this one; one look at that nose that was using Daffodil's face for a perch and a nitwit would know why the third generation of Hyman Brills had skedaddled. That left the mystery of why he'd hooked up with her in the first place, and just how Lyon was going to twist Delmer Warp from client to criminal overlord.

It all gave me palpitations, as at a nod from the boss I swiveled to my processor and prepared to take notes on the conference. Was this the case that would jar him out of his delusional lifestyle, preparing him for a sane existence and me for unemployment? The only fly in our cushy ointment, Gus's and mine, was that a sudden attack of compos mentis would strike our Dutch uncle, forcing us to become contributing members of society.

I tucked my fear aside long enough to record the details of the happy couple's sudden separation and Lyon's subsequent cross-examination of the bride. Her father held her hand throughout the ordeal, patting it from time to time and interrupting the stream of questions to interject a phrase or a sentence. Her other hand wore a wedding set the size of matched life preservers, glittering with sparklers. His accent hovered somewhere between Bela Lugosi and Boris Badenov, while she spoke pure Kentucky cornpone, all "you-all" this and "you-all" that.

I expected Lyon to grill her over whether Brill was as well-off as the society page made out, or had latched onto the daughter of the undertaker-turned-furniture-baron for her fortune, only to quail at the thought of having to wake up to that proboscis every morning for the rest of his life; but that would have been too rational. Instead he pumped her for information on the nature of her husband's acquaintances, until it dawned on me that he suspected Brill had been kidnapped and that she would hear from his abductors any time with a ransom demand.

Eventually he shifted his focus to the father. I hit a couple of clinkers on the keyboard when he began hammering on Warp's business picture; the fat little salmon was swimming upstream in a mad dash to prove that the trade in coffee tables and Barcalounger had gone soft and that the father of the bride had had his son-in-law snatched in order to extort money from Hyman Brill Jr., the venture capitalist, in return for the safe delivery of his son.

But Warp, underworld genius or no, tumbled to that line of reasoning a split second before I did, gathered up his daughter, and stormed out of the room, leaving Lyon's face in a self-satisfied pout and—shocking me to the lisle socks I could only afford because he was careless about keeping up with the household accounts—his left finger doing a do-si-do inside the ear on that side of his Charlie Brown–shaped head with his eyes closed in rapture.

He only did that when he was about to come up with a solution that addressed every point of conjecture. It was his equivalent of Nero Wolfe pursing and drawing in his lips just before he separated a fat rabbit from a silk hat.

"If you're thinking of railroading our client," I said, "you might as well call Captain Stoddard and give him the good news. As much as he'd like to nail us both for playing detective without a ticket, he'll be grateful for a front-row seat in civil court when Warp sues you for false accusation, defamation of character, and a bad case of cholesterol on the brain."

He wasn't listening—not because he had one ear stopped up, but because when he went into one of those trances it could last for minutes or hours while the world spun merrily away outside his notice. I got up.

"So long to you, Porky. I'm going to propose to Daffodil Warp-Brill, and beat the rush when the annulment comes through. Maybe her old man will make me vice president in charge of the wicker division."

His eyes popped open and he withdrew the finger. "Don't be obtuse, Arnie. No annulment is necessary. However, you would have to wait for a divorce, an event I fear is unlikely."

"If we're going to split hairs over legal definitions, let's talk slander, false and malicious accusation, violation—"

"I wasn't referring to the dissolution of the Brills' marriage. That would be unnecessary, since it was never legal to begin with. She was already married when they walked down the aisle."

"To who?" Well, I suppose it should have been "To whom"; but I was too rattled to bone up on posh.

"To Delmer Warp. He has no daughter. Daffodil is his wife."

"Everyone knows you're nuttier than a Whitman's Sampler, but this time you've gone to the front of the line at Bellevue. Those noses came from the same genetic code."

"People are often attracted to one another by a shared physical trait; also, there's something to be said for the theory that in time, couples acquire a resemblance. Didn't you notice the way he held her hand all the time I was bearing down on her? Did that look like the way a father holds his daughter's hand, at least in a normal parent-child relationship? You're a keener observer than that. But in case you did miss it, surely you noticed the strong trace of his Lithuanian origins in his pronunciation, while the woman's speech came directly from a Kentucky coal mine."

"I thought maybe she had a Southern-fried mother."

"Indeed." He was actually bouncing in his chair; try as he did to stay in character, his natural enthusiasm for his make-believe sometimes trumped Wolfe's gravitas. "How old did you determine her to be?"

"Thirty, thirty-five; although the front of her face might have preceded the rest of her by a year."

"Delmer Warp could pass for sixty, but a corrupt soul ages at an accelerated rate. He observed his fortieth birthday last May. I read of the event in the company newsletter. His business is incorporated, and I happen to own a share of stock. I know you think I've exaggerated his gifts, but I cannot accuse him of embracing parenthood at five or ten years of age. I can only conclude that your head was too full of dollar signs to see anything but the lucrative case Warp had chosen to dangle before us."

I lashed back. "I was distracted by that meatball on her wedding finger. A man could live—"

"Not for a day on paste like that. I might have been taken in myself for a minute at least. Genuine jewelry that size resides only in the Tower of London; but it had to be large enough to cover the pale spot where she's worn a wedding ring for years, or draw suspicion to so recently married a finger. Once that explanation occurred to me, the rest was child's play."

I sat back, blowing air. "Well, butter my—"

He glanced at the clock and rose. "Speaking of butter, Gus will be serving his commendable goulash in three minutes."

"But what was Warp after?"

"Come, come, Arnie. Dining, digestion, disclosure. In that order."

Later, settling himself back behind the carrier-class desk and burping paprika, he answered my question.

"You heard me asking Warp about his business. Surely you saw I suspected him of not being as successful as the *Garden State Gazette* made him out to be. What you could not have known is that I was positive, based upon his last quarter as it appeared in the stockholders' report.

"In the daily columns, every heiress is beautiful, and every prominent entrepreneur a major captain of industry. It sells copies. Well, you've met the heiress. Warp overbought maple bedroom sets last year following a retirement home epidemic, just before the bottom dropped out of that market. He's inventory-heavy and cash-poor. In order to get out from under, he fobbed off his wife on the son of a genuine tycoon, hoping to blackmail him into making a handsome settlement to avoid being accused of bigamy. I assume she has charms that weren't evident in her current circumstances.

"Hyman Brill Jr. is a recluse. He's rarely been photographed, and he pays a reverse publicity agent to keep his name out of the press. I doubt he was pleased even to see it connected with his son's blessed event. To fight the accusation would drag out the affair, bringing entertainment to thousands of people at his expense. He'll pay—unless we get in touch with him and give him the score, so he can threaten Warp before Warp can threaten him. No doubt the element of surprise will frighten Warp into inaction, sparing Brill effort."

I've been over it and over it—just in case there was something in it for me—but it always comes out as loony as a Canadian dollar. Lyon had made some sharp observations, but the rest was wild speculation based on his certainty that Delmer Warp was Genghis Khan in a suit. Okay, a few days later a two-line note appeared in the *Gazette* to the effect that the Brill-Warp marriage had been dissolved "by mutual consent." It didn't make the little stump right, but it didn't make him wrong, either. That's the advantage of being cuckoo: You can't prove sanity without eliminating evidence of derangement, and one man's dementia is another man's quaint quirk.

And when you *had* him pegged as a paranoid-schizo with delusions of normalcy, he reached up his sleeve and dealt you a hand you couldn't beat; which is what he did that afternoon in his office.

He chuckled, ending on a squeak. "Warp panicked when young Brill vanished. He thought he'd seen through his nefarious plot, and wanted to find him and convince him otherwise before he had a chance to report to his father."

I'd never heard anyone use "nefarious" out loud before; but I let it drift. "Is that why Brill Three scrammed? He doped it out himself?"

"I doubt it. Anyone who'd fall for so transparent a ruse would be unlikely to see the light on his own."

"Why, then?"

He opened *And Be a Villain* to the strip of bacon. "You surprise me. You saw that nose. No man who didn't daily face the identical feature in a mirror could put up with it. I thought you of all people would be shallow enough to see that."

PETER AND THE WOLFE

"As one loony to another, you might be able to shake this guy's story and get him to cough up his real moniker."

The moon turned blue, swine flew, and hell sprouted icicles.

Mind you, I can't swear to these things. Brooklynites never look at the sky, and having spent time in stir, I'd rather not find out for sure if things are worse down below; but when Captain Stoddard of the NYPD calls up Claudius Lyon to ask for his services as a detective, you can be sure that all of the above is gospel.

Lyon himself never answers the phone when either Gus, the keeper of the keys, or I'm around. Nero Wolfe doesn't, and his worshipper across the river wouldn't tie his shoes without confirming which loop Wolfe makes longer. (Not that the little lump would bend over regardless.) So when the bell rang during his morning two hours in the office, I picked up the receiver. "Claudius Lyon's office. Arnie Woodbine speaking."

The boss, watching me over the Nancy Drew coloring book, registered alarm at my reaction to the voice scraping in my ear. "Arnie, are you having an aneurysm?"

I might as well have been; they say it's impossible to answer yes to that question, and I could no sooner have identified who was on the other end of the line than I could have removed my foot from the third rail in the subway. I inclined my no-doubt pallid face toward the extension on the desk.

Wherever it was my blood had gone, Lyon's joined it when Stoddard yelped at him. It would make the captain's year if he nailed one or both of us for conducting private investigations without a license. No matter that there were worse crimes to address; they weren't personal. He likes us the way suede likes rain, the way mongooses like cobras, the way Krazy Kat likes bricks. He don't like us, is what I'm saying. I kept my receiver to my ear. I was afraid he'd hear the click if I hung up, and rubber-hose me for rudeness.

"Mr. Stoddard," Lyon squeaked. "To what do I owe this—"

"Take that sentence where it's going and I'll reach down this wire with both hands and rip your lungs out through your nose. Did you read today's *Tattler*?"

Which showed he kept up on his homework. Lyon's addicted to that local scandal sheet, with its aliens in the White House, pig-faced boys, and a legitimate news item when it runs out of freaks. At a look from my employer I got the morning edition out of the drawer of my desk where I store slugs for the parking meter, snapped it open, and scanned through the Elvis sightings until I found something that seemed to serve. I folded to the short piece and passed it across the big desk. It ran:

JOHN DOE THINKS HE'S SAINT

Brooklyn, December 5: Yesterday, local police
took into custody a man found wandering down the
middle of Ocean Parkway who police say has identified
himself only as Saint Peter, traditionally known as
the custodian of the pearly gates to heaven.
So far, according to Captain Stoddard of the
Eleventh Precinct, attempts to learn the man's true
identity have proven . . .

Now, nothing short of a chocolate éclair the size of his head can restore Lyon's composure faster than a fresh mystery to solve. That's what Wolfe does all the time, and what I said about tying his shoelaces applies quadruply to detecting. He even rediscovered his sense of humor. "I assume, sir," he said, "you're referring to the counterfeit apostle you have locked up in a cell and not this other item about the captain of the SS *Titanic* located alive and well on a desert island; although it does pique my interest that the commander of a vessel that went down in the North Atlantic in 1912 should resurface on an atoll in the Pacific."

Precedents were falling everywhere that morning. Not only did Stoddard not follow through on his promise to separate Lyon from his lungs; he responded in a tone I suppose a snarling Doberman would consider polite. "I wish I had that one. The department shrink and every colleague he can dredge up to consult can't shake this character's story. He's Saint Peter, that's that, and my thirty-year record's shot to sh—"

"How can I assist you?" It was just as much of a novelty for the boss to interrupt the captain in mid-gripe as for the captain to let him; but Lyon dislikes profanity. "Phooey" is as close as he ever comes, far as it is from Wolfe's "Pfui." My fat little meal ticket also disapproves of spraying saliva.

"It came to me we've been going about this all wrong. They say it takes a thief to catch a thief. I've proved that's malarkey, but one nut sure enough knows how to talk fruitcake. As one loony to another, you might be able to shake this guy's story and get him to cough up his real moniker."

At this point I'd recovered myself enough to put in my shekel's worth. "Excuse me, Captain, but there's only one mental deficient in this conversation. I'm not the sharpest blade in the shop, but I'm sane, and Mrs. Woodbine didn't raise her children to fall for a sure case of entrapment. Mr. Lyon solves your little conundrum, you're so grateful for the commendation you get from the chief you hand him one of your four-for-a-quarter stogies, and the second he claps his squat fingers around it you bust him for accepting a fee for practicing without a license."

"You, too, as an accomplice. But this is on the level. If he manages to pull this off—and I'm grasping at straws here, fat as this one is; I think he's a dumb cluck with dumb luck, and sure as hell when it runs out it'll be when he's working for me—I won't even give him so much as a thank you."

"That part I buy," I said. "The 'no thanks' part. Nice try, Captain. Try again some other—"

I saved my breath too late. I was looking at the chub on the other side of that Olympic-regulation-sized desk, and from his expression you'd have thought he was Popeye and Captain Stoddard was a can of spinach.

"Lunch is served in one hour," he said. "You and Saint Peter are invited to share Gus's superb matzo ball soup."

I waited until the receiver banged—even when he wasn't ticked off at us, which was mostly always, Stoddard never broke off a conversation without making an angry racket—then got up from my chair. Lyon glanced at the clock. "Where are you going? I have germination records to dictate."

"The tomatoes can germinate themselves, which is what they do anyway. You're not fooling anybody with those four hours a day you waste up there. I've got some vacation days coming and I'm taking them now. When I get back from Vegas, I'll visit you in the hoosegow. I may even have Gus whip up a herring with a saw in it."

"Don't be absurd. The last time you visited Las Vegas you had to hitchhike back. You pawned your return ticket and lost everything on a hand of stud."

"It was Texas Hold'em; and I'd sooner work my way back washing dishes in every greasy spoon between here and Reno than press shirts in a prison laundry. I've done both, so I'm not just talking through my hat."

"Nonsense. We have Mr. Stoddard's word it isn't coggery."

I had to lean over my keyboard to look up that one: The man wouldn't step out of character long enough even to use something simple like *deception*. "If you were half the detective you think you are, and Wolfe was half the detective you think he is—which makes you a quarter of a detective, and even that only in your own mind—

you'd know that the law against lying to a cop don't work both ways. He'd lie on a gallon of truth serum if he thought he could cogger you into the joint."

"You know I detest it when you turn a noun into a verb. Sit down, confound it! If it comes to that, I'll confess and exonerate you into the bargain."

It just so happens that Lyon is as good as his word, nutty as he is; so I took my seat and blew off the rest of the morning taking down blather from *Gardening for Dummies* until Gus's gong and then the doorbell rang, announcing lunch and our guests.

⚜

I was disappointed. I'd anticipated a beard you could lose a shoe in, sandals, and a white robe, which was what I would have expected if there was some clerical error and I ever actually stood before the gates to Paradise. Stoddard's companion could use a shave—could have used it last week, in fact—but it was more stubble than flow, and his rusty sports coat, yellowing collar, grubby jeans, and scuffed brogans slashed at the toes to let the corns breathe would have turned him away from any restaurant in Brooklyn, if not the eye of the needle. He smelled of the can, as well as of the alley behind Skipper Dan's House of Fish on Day-Old Saturday. Carbon-dating being out of the question, I pegged him as somewhere between fifty and nine hundred and sixty-nine; or was that Methuselah? I'm rusty on the Old Testament. If there was any hope for me at all, it was grounded in the Gospels.

"Okay if I call you Saint?" I asked our distinguished visitor.

He said nothing. He looked as patient as one, I'd say that for him. Stoddard said, "He don't exactly talk your ear off. All we can get out of him is his name, and it ain't even that."

"Saint Peter," said our guest. Flat vowels: Chicago?

"See?"

Entering the dining room we found Claudius Lyon exactly where anyone who read Archie Goodwin's accounts of Nero Wolfe's investigations would expect him at that hour, rooted at the head of the long table with utensils at the ready. Upon our appearance, he did something almost without precedent; although if it were entirely so in Wolfe's case, he'd never have considered it. He hopped to his feet and inclined his chins in a gesture of respect. "Sir, you are welcome in my home. Please be seated at my right hand."

In response to the tilt of a puffy palm, Stoddard's charge took possession of the honored place; gaining his host no points with the captain, who like Wolfe's Inspector Cramer considered himself the guest of honor at any gathering, even one ostensibly social. Knowing how well the chief of Brooklyn Bunco took disappointment, I hoped the boss wouldn't slip his trolley the rest of the way and forget his promise to give me a clean slate when the axe came down.

Stoddard seized one of the chairs reserved for the unanointed and stuck a Lucky between his teeth, without lighting it. He chewed a pack a day.

"Since the New York Police Department won't, allow me to apologize to you for your detainment. Apart from worrying some of our fellow citizens in regard to your safety, you've committed no offense."

"Loitering," Stoddard growled. "Disturbing the peace."

"The U.S. Supreme Court has found the charge of loitering unconstitutional under the First Amendment. As to the other, I don't concede that causing concern regarding one's welfare belongs to the same category as shouting obscenities in public or playing a radio too loud."

"Vagrancy, then. He hasn't a penny on him."

"Nor do I; nor does the queen of England, or for that matter anyone who depends on credit, which is most of us. Come now, Mr. Stoddard. I suggest you release this man."

"Even your precious Constitution says I can hold him for forty-eight hours without charging him."

"Muleheaded."

"What?" A cigarette got bit through.

Lyon paled, but was spared worse by the arrival of Gus, who ladled out the soup. We dined in silence for a quarter-hour. Even Stoddard, who'd read up on the Wolfe canon in order to lay a snare for his imitator, put up with the master's rule against discussing business during a meal. When the dishes were cleared away, we returned to the office, where Lyon compounded the insult to the captain by offering the man in his custody the comfort of the orange leather chair facing the desk. I gave the little glob of wax points for chutzpah. Maybe the captain's new status of client as opposed to mortal enemy had put some lead in his pencil. Stoddard took it, in any case; although it cost him the price of a fresh cigarette to replace the one he'd gnawed to bits. He threw himself into one of the green chairs.

Lyon addressed his companion. "Returning to the subject of our precious Constitution: You're entitled to an attorney, if you wish, at no cost to you."

"Saint Peter" said nothing. He didn't even shake his head.

"If he'd opened his mouth to ask, he'd've got one," was all Stoddard said.

"No doubt you informed him. You must be bored," he told our honored guest. "In lieu of the distraction of conversation, might I offer you something to read? The Bible, perhaps. I take the liberty of assuming it's high on your list."

Nothing again. We got more comment out of Lyon's blasted tomatoes.

Lyon leaned forward in his seat; and damned if I didn't see a gleam in those little pig's eyes. "Forgive me. It never crossed my mind that perhaps you can't read."

A tectonic plate moved under the rock that supported greater New York; a snowball formed in hell, a politician told the truth, and "Saint Peter" opened his mouth.

"Sure I can read. Think I'm stupid?"

"By God!" Stoddard plucked out his Lucky and threw it into a corner. "Why didn't you say something before this?"

I smirked. "'Up till now everything's been all right.'" Facing the captain's black face, I felt my own grow white. "Sorry. Old joke."

"I apologize." Lyon was still addressing the man in the orange chair. "Sometimes you have to prick someone's vanity to get him to open up. No Bible, then."

"Anything but."

At most times, the man seated in the preposterously huge chair behind the preposterously huge desk looked like a little boy sitting in his father's place on Take Your Child to Work Day. When, however, he sat back and rotated an index finger in one ear, he filled both chair and desk. It meant, as surely as Wolfe's lips pushing out and pulling back in, that he had something solid to work on at last. He was coaxing oxygen into the tight whorls in his brain to wake up the gray cells.

I'd seen him at that for hours or minutes, and was prepared to suffer any abuse from Stoddard, corseted as he was by his new role as customer, when Lyon removed his finger and wiped it delicately with a green silk handkerchief. To "Saint Peter": "Forgive me if I ask something personal. Your parents weren't very religious, were they?"

"That's putting it mildly." Now that he'd gone beyond three syllables, I definitely noticed the Chicago accent. "My mother called herself an agnostic, but my father was more direct. 'Thank God I'm an atheist.' It was his favorite joke."

"Then why in God's name—if you'll excuse the expression—did they name you Saint Peter?"

"Peter's the family name. I guess they thought by naming their boy Saint they were putting one over on the devout. I'd have told that to this nimrod, if he'd given me the chance. The minute I gave him my name he thought I was crazy."

He chuckled then, and drew a dirty cuff across his lips when saliva trickled out. "I sure wasn't about to give him any satisfaction beyond that. Meanwhile I got three hots and a cot, and all at the expense of the NYPD."

"So you're not the man who decides who lets whom in through the gates of Heaven."

"If there's anything to it, I guess the man who does will understand." Saint Peter cut a look at Stoddard. "*You* might have some explaining to do."

Lyon frowned at the fuming Stoddard. "You have no grounds for keeping this man in custody. Far from obstructing justice, he's cooperated with it in every way, including providing it with his true identity."

The captain's face worked; then a grin broke loose, like the sun poking its way through storm clouds. He rose from his chair. "You're right. Thanks again for the feed. Here's a little something for your next." He drew a can of oysters from his vest pocket and stuck it across the desk.

Lyon kept his hands under the top. "Thank you, but Gus's religion prohibits eating or serving shellfish."

Saint Peter declined the offer of cab fare, explaining as he stood that he was within walking distance of a shelter he enjoyed. By that time Stoddard was long gone, with the evidence against Lyon back in his pocket.

"You were right, Arnie," Lyon said. "I was naive. Mr. Stoddard tried to rope us after all. I have his ignorance of the Hebrew faith to thank for my salvation. And your counsel, of course. I should have known you'd spot a man's dishonesty where I could not."

I wasn't sure how to take that; being a crook gives you the same advantage over both an honest and a dishonest man, but how a fruitcake thinks is anyone's guess.

"How'd you know he was on the level and that his name was really Saint Peter?"

"Mr. Stoddard said it best. An insane man knows insanity when he sees it, and when he does not. Clearly the fellow was telling the truth. At a guess, the blasphemy of his christening offered no compunctions to his parents, hence the assumption that they were not believers. Once I asked myself if his name was as reported, the rest was simplicity itself." He sighed. "To the devious man, like our friend the captain, there is nothing so obscure as the obvious."

Whereupon he laid aside the weighty tome on his desk and picked up Mary Higgins Clark with a happy little sigh.

WOLFE WHISTLE

"I never get to travel first class with anyone sane."

Claudius Lyon must stay awake nights reading Archie Goodwin's reports of his employer's adventures just to bone up on WWND (What Would Nero Do—or not do?); God forbid that he should take some action or say anything that his personal saint might find unacceptable. His whole life is a final exam. It wears out my brain just thinking about it—but not to the point where I hand in my notice. A crackpot with unlimited funds is to a grifter like me what an aging eccentric rich childless widow is to her cat. All I have to do is humor him, curl up from time to time with *Fer-de-Lance* or *Too Many Cooks* or *The Mother Hunt* for a Goodwin refresher course, and it's silk sheets and three squares for me for as long as I can manage to keep my meal ticket out of a butterfly net.

Oh, and split what I skim off the household accounts with Gus, Lyon's major-domo and the best kosher chef in Brooklyn, at least according to *The Gus Book of World Records*.

Call me Arnie, or Mr. Woodbine if you like. Just don't call me 67024, which is what I answered to in Sing Sing after a misunderstanding with the NYPD.

Crooks of my type are level-headed by nature, so why a man who has enough loose screws of his own would borrow more from someone else has me stumped. My guy has an unreasoning fear of chimpanzees, so I had to lock out the Animal Planet channel. Wolfe so far as I know has no such phobia, but his dislike of venturing out of his brownstone cocoon in Manhattan is an issue Goodwin deals with on a regular basis. Corned beef is banned from Wolfe's kitchen, barbecue of any kind from Lyon's; both Goodwin and I have to go out after such delicacies when the craving strikes. The fat man across the bridge considers yellow the superior color in the spectrum, and if Lyon hangs one more pair of green curtains under his roof or moves in another piece of green upholstery, our home sweet home will look as if it was decorated by Kermit the Frog.

There are places where the boss's predispositions match Wolfe's, without masquerading: Both men are fat (though I suspect Lyon's five-foot-nothing height would hardly support his hero's infamous "seventh of a ton"), both solve puzzles placed before them by outsiders, and I think Lyon's fear of riding in moving vehicles surpasses even the master's.

But if anything about such travel gives him a five-alarm case of the shakes, it's the possibility of missing his ride. I doubt I could get him on an airplane without a chloroform rag, but when his car gets stuck in cross-town traffic on the way to pick him up or—as in the case of what I'm about to relate—he has a ticket to board a specific train at a prearranged time, I'd as soon sing "Brahms' Lullaby" to a swarm of bees as try to calm him down.

The North American Chapter of the International Tomato-Growers Association was holding its annual convention in Youngstown, Ohio. The event was important enough to ink in, as a nod to one of Wolfe's rare excursions outside the city. As Lyon put it, "I feel it my responsibility as a demonstration of good faith to attend the mother group and show solidarity against the upstarts."

See, growing orchids (you-know-who's hobby) is a challenge to the most expert horticulturists, and impossible for anyone with a thumb as brown as Lyon's; but as he can't let his roof stand empty during the hours his role model tends his flowers, he grows tomatoes, which if you just leave them on their own will grow themselves. But ever since a rift in the ITGA had led to the formation of a rebel establishment calling itself the Western Tomato Growers Society, Lyon had thrown in heart, soul, and blubber with the legitimate original. He was an officer of some kind in an honorary capacity, and mounted his certificate in a frame on his office wall next to a portrait of Lester Broadacre, the botanist who introduced the tomatillo to the United States. Of course I was to accompany him to the event, which I looked forward to with the eager anticipation of an amateur colonoscopy.

"I don't see why we had to put our fate in the hands of a taxi driver," he said, when we started away from the curb with our bags overflowing the trunk into the back seat: Three days and three nights in foreign territory required he travel as heavily as Count Dracula with his boxes of earth. "Is that the face of a terrorist or is it not?" He pointed a sausage-shaped finger at the cabby's ID. His name was Maurice Feinstein.

"Not unless he plans to blow up a Bob Evans," I said. "Relax, boss. We'll be at trackside an hour before our train."

"Now you're tempting the forces of darkness. There will be a strike, or an accident, or he'll take us to the wrong place."

"It's Grand Central Station. He can't miss it."

He didn't, of course; but Lyon fretted over every piece of luggage the redcap loaded aboard his cart and scrutinized the man's uniform, which he was convinced he'd stolen, leaving the rightful owner bound and gagged in his underwear in an equipment room. We caught our train with plenty of time to spare. I sat back, but before I could breathe a prayer of thanks for relief, he took a small square box from his overcoat pocket and laid it on my thigh.

"If it's valium," I said, "you should keep one for yourself. Better make it a half-dozen, just to be sure."

"Open it."

I jerked loose the ribbon and lifted the lid. A silver-plated whistle glittered inside on a chain.

"Put it on. I want you to keep an eye on the time, and blow it two hours before our train leaves for home. These affairs can be loud. I might miss a word of warning, and I cannot imagine a worse experience than to have to spend another day in Youngstown, Ohio."

"Try spending one day with you in Brooklyn," I muttered.

"What?"

"I said I forgot to bring my copy of Huck Finn, to read on the train." I hung the chain around my neck and poked the whistle under my shirt. Next he'd have me sewing his name in his underwear.

But, hey: I never get to travel first class with anyone sane.

⚜

We reached our destination without derailing or running into a single cow, despite Lyon's dire predictions, and alighted from our cab with him no nearer hysteria than when confronted by our mortal enemy, Bunco Squad Captain Stoddard; I, however, wished that box *had* contained something more calming than a police whistle. Maintaining repose in the presence of a companion who jumps out of his socks every time the car sways around a bend takes character. Which I have not any of. The sign outside the convention center hotel was like a pardon from the governor:

WELCOME DELEGATES

TO THE NORTH AMERICAN CHAPTER OF THE ITGA

I won't belabor my dozens of readers with details of the schedule. As promising as a panel entitled "The Seductive History of *Lycopersicum esculentum* (Part One)" might sound, or "One Hour with a Legend: A Conversation with Sir Pearson Childroot, Father of the Modern Piccalilli," I'll guide you past the meeting rooms to the exhibition hall. There, among such wonders as a plant crossbred from the plum, cherry, and pear varieties of the Ecuadorian tomato, a demonstration of a revolutionary new scientific method of canning the common beefsteak, and a placard advertising an autograph party that evening featuring Mildred Cuddy, author of *Ketchup or Catsup? A Guide for the Beginner*, the largest and most jabbery crowd had gathered around a small square glass box mounted on a deep metal case, containing a terra cotta pot with something that looked like a gargantuan blueberry squatting at the end of a curly vine.

"*Lycopersicum rumplicus*," announced its breeder, Rear Admiral (ret.) Barton Rumple, "is the product of more than thirty years of experimentation, and no doubt contributed to my decision to leave the navy," he said, showing tobacco-stained teeth behind a snow-white mustache. "But I think the result more than bears out the sacrifice."

"What's it taste like?" I asked.

A cold eye as blue as his exhibit regarded me. Erect in his dark blue suit, pressed stiff as aluminum siding, he might have been preparing to argue a point of strategy with John Paul Jones. Then again came that brittle yellow smile. "I have no idea. I forced this first specimen in time to display at this event, then fretted lest it overripen before the unveiling. After all that, I clean forgot to slice it up and fix myself a BLT to eat on the road."

Laughter rippled through his admirers. The loudest and most high-pitched came from Lyon, who by now I knew was gearing up to beg for a favor, making a spectacle of himself and anyone associated with him.

But it wasn't until a reception in the hospitality suite an hour later that the boss got Rumple alone.

"A triumph, Admiral! Truly the finest specimen I've seen since Herbert Lydecker unveiled the floating trellis in nineteen sixty-nine."

Rumple snorted and stirred a vodka tonic with his swizzle. "Lydecker was a rough carpenter, not a botanist. Any fool can prevent a plant from rotting on the ground."

"True, true." Lyon nodded, and went on nodding as if he'd forgotten how to stop. I wanted to shake him till his fat head rolled off his shoulders. Instead I gulped Scotch. He went on: "I wonder if you might share with me your breeding process?"

Which as I could have predicted bought him the stink eye worse than when I'd suggested the heresy of actually eating his damn fruit.

"You're that Wolfe fellow, aren't you?"

"Claudius Lyon. He and I are in the same profession."

"Well, Mr. Lyon, if you're half the detective they say Wolfe is, perhaps you can figure it out yourself."

"Phooey!" spat Lyon, when the admiral boated off toward a refreshment table laid out with cold cuts, finger treats, and sliced cheese and garnished with tomatoes in every color but blue. "I have half a mind to take him up on the challenge! Thirty years indeed! What did he do with the rest of the time, put ships in bottles?"

"I'd start by looking for that half a mind," I said into my glass.

"What?"

I pointed at the table. "I said, 'Look! Pickled watermelon rind!'"

⚜

We had adjoining rooms. Before retiring to mine, I reported to his for instructions. At his invitation I entered to find him in bed, propped up with pillows and with the spread drawn up over his belly, which looked as if he'd smuggled a watermelon from the kitchen; the bilious green pajama jacket only added to the illusion. "First thing in the morning, Arnie, call the concierge and have a large floral display delivered to Admiral Rumple's room. Spare no expense. This on the card: 'Congratulations again upon your momentous discovery, and thank you for listening to my proposition. Meanwhile, please consider me if you should ever have need for an investigator. I'm sure we can come to an agreement that pleases us both. Yours most sincerely, etc.'"

I typed this treacle into my iPad, nearly punching my fingers through the other side. "You're wasting your time, not to mention the florist's, and making more of a fool of yourself than usual, if that's possible. He's taking that recipe with him to his grave, and welcome to it. Personally I'd rather eat green eggs and ham than something that should be hanging on a Christmas tree."

"It's a process, not a recipe. Is that clock right? Check your watch against it. Have you your whistle?"

"I left it in my room. Our train doesn't leave till day after tomorrow."

"Keep it on you at all times. Nothing short of carrying away a cutting from *Lycopersicum rumplicus* under my arm would compensate me for missing it."

I wished to heaven I'd had it. Maybe blasting it in his ear would shock him back into his normal state of lunacy.

⚜

The next day we skipped the program and paid another visit to Rumple's blue tomato. Most of the attendees were packed in to the main auditorium listening to a lecture on the threat posed by the Asian hornworm, so we had the exhibit all to ourselves. Lyon studied the specimen in the glass case from all sides, finally raising himself on tiptoe to peer down through the top.

"Note the time, Arnie."

"We've still got till tomorrow; and yes, I'm wearing the damn whistle."

"I don't mean that."

I looked at my watch. "Eight ten A.M."

"Do you recall what time it was when we first laid eyes on this remarkable hybrid?"

As a matter of fact I did. One of the few good qualities I share with Wolfe's Goodwin is a good memory; it came from studying undercover cops' faces so one doesn't take the same fall at the same hands twice. "Seven P.M., give or take a minute."

A row of windows looked out on the sun shining down on the Mahoning River. He squinted that way, shielding his eyes with a hand. "Interesting."

"Not really."

A convention volunteer moved among the displays, covering them with yards of blue cloth. When he got to ours, he excused himself and said the room was closing until after the morning sessions. We left him draping the miraculous tomato plant and went to breakfast in the restaurant, where for one morning in my life I got the taste of Gus's lox and bagels out of my mouth. We'd finished eating and I was browsing the race results on my iPad over coffee when he said, "What kind of information can you look up on that gadget?"

Lyon has raised Luddism to the level of art. He'd given up limiting me to a manual typewriter—any technology not mentioned in the Wolfe canon was moonshine—only because I'd worn out two dictionaries trying to spell his favorite words. I said, "Sure. Can you say the same thing for an Underwood?"

"Never mind that. Instructions."

In the past, using my laptop back home, I'd extracted information for him on everything from Revelation to root rot, all without raising an eyebrow; but this time it seemed like make-work. I didn't get to ask what it was about, though, because just when I finished reporting, Admiral Rumple came galloping up to our table. "Mr. Lyon! I tried calling your room. I'm so glad I caught you."

Lyon beamed, snatched his napkin from under his collar, and wiped his hands. "I take it the flowers came. Think nothing—"

"Oh, blast the flowers! Did you mean what you said in the note?"

"Certainly! About our coming to an agreement? Certainly!"

His excited squeak belonged to Minnie Mouse.

Rumple said, "Yes, yes! You may have the secret to *Lycopersicum rumplicus*, if only you can restore it to me. I can't duplicate it without a cutting from the existing plant."

Lyon asked no questions, but hopped down from his seat and we accompanied the admiral to the display room. We were hard-pressed to keep up with him, Lyon on his plump little legs and me wondering how fast an old wheeze can run without blowing an artery.

We found the place even more abuzz than the evening before, and the crowd around the admiral's glass case even denser. With the military man forcing his way through, we came up to stare at the empty case.

"I got here right after the attendant lifted the cover for the afternoon viewing," Rumple said. "It was as you see it now. Someone managed to get in and steal the plant while the rest of us were absent! Lyon, if you're a patch on your idol in the detecting game—"

"Nothing is to be gained from panic. I assume the plant is insured?"

"For five hundred thousand dollars; but it's worth far more than that to me. It represents the culmination of my life's work outside the navy."

"You agree to my terms?"

"Yes, yes! I will deliver to you all the records on the *Lycopersicum rumplicus* breeding process the moment the plant is restored to me unharmed."

"Satisfactory."

I'd expected the little toad to turn a cartwheel, but instead he stuck a finger in his left ear and started rotating it. When Lyon's brain gets into gear, the wax in that appendage doesn't stand a chance.

This time he was at it less than ten seconds. His gaze sought the attendant we'd spoken to that morning. "Who had access to this room while the exhibit was closed?"

"Just the hotel staff, myself included. But we were under Admiral Rumple's strict orders not to attempt to open the case or even move it. He installed it himself."

"Installed; I approve of your vocabulary, young man. Was the admiral present when you uncovered the case this afternoon?"

"No, sir. No one but staff was admitted until the room was reopened to the public. That was when I saw the case was empty."

"You called security, of course."

"I insisted," Rumple broke in. "I came in as soon as the doors opened, and when I found out what had happened, I made the call myself from the house phone."

"I responded to the call."

The man who spoke wasn't in uniform, but he might as well have had RENT-A-COP tattooed on his forehead. I'd cased enough places to spot that institutional blue suit and matching tie-and-handkerchief set across a department store. His face was another clue: straight from the mail-order catalog and as expressionless as a Parker House roll. The walkie-talkie on his belt only confirmed it.

"Officer, I want you to detain this man for the police." Lyon inclined his head toward Rumple, whose face turned as red as the brightest fruit on display. But before he could speak: "Spare yourself, Admiral, the ordeal of accusing me of a jest, a show of outrage, and the threat of a lawsuit. I came here without a specimen worthy of an exhibit, but I rather think I can participate."

Suddenly he grasped the glass case between his palms and snatched it up from the table. Hugging it under one arm, he found a catch on the black metal base and manipulated it. A drawer slid out containing something that looked like a miniature crystal ball mounted on a circuit board.

"Mr. Woodbine will attest that I live unencumbered by contemporary technology," he said; "but I read; and what I've read emboldens me to theorize that this equipment is intended to project the holographic image of, say, a blue tomato, inside a glass case, on a battery charge designed to last at least three days; long enough, in any event, to satisfy those attending this convention that what they regarded as a living exhibit was genuine."

"Holograph?" asked the guard.

"Surely everyone today is familiar with three-dimensional imagery." Lyon swept his gaze across the sea of goggle-eyed faces. "Fellow horticulturists, it grieves me to inform you that the *Lycopersicum rumplicus* does not exist. It never did. If Rumple hasn't destroyed it, you will likely find its original, counterfeited through a computerized process from the lowly beefsteak, to represent the unique blue variety he subjected to enhancement.

"What is the old term for similar chicanery?" he asked. "'Smoke and mirrors'?"

Rumple's face had passed through its own computerized process, changing colors several times. Now it was as dark as the loam that Lyon had imported semiannually from the Brazilian rainforest at a cost of twice what I'd nicked from him all year, all to grow his damn love apples. "You're on thin ice, you fat fraud. You can't prove any of this."

"When the police search you, I feel certain they'll find a remote control that operates the miniature projector installed in the bottom of this case. If not, it will turn up in your room. All you had to do in order to make it appear that your plant had been stolen was switch it off, then collect half a million dollars from your insurance company."

He looked at me. "My associate is in a position to expedite the investigation. His marvelous electronic pocket device has supplied us both with the admiral's biography, which by reason of his taxpayer-paid salary is in the public domain, barring certain details labeled secret in the interest of national security; I trust Mr. Woodbine has saved the data. Rumple spent most of his career at the Pentagon, researching weapons development. His department spent a great deal of time studying holographic photography. Is it too much to suppose that its intention was to project a nonexistent armada upon any harbor in the world, diverting enemy attention from where our real naval forces are actually gathering?"

An experienced military officer knows when he's beaten. When the police came to search him, he made no resistance, and showed no reaction when a cigar-shaped object was taken from his inside breast pocket. It had one button only, marked POWER. When it was pressed, the blue tomato returned, looking as real as ever. One of the cops read him his rights.

"Boss," I said as they took him away in handcuffs, "I have to hand it—"

"Phooey!" Lyon spun on his heel and waddled out, plowing a path through his fellow tomato-fanciers.

I followed him, wanting to tell him to look at the bright side: If the dingus was genuine and he'd collected on Rumple's promise to show him how to grow one of his own, Captain Stoddard back in Brooklyn would've called it payment for investigative services and clinked him for operating without a license, which he'd been trying to do for years. But I knew it wouldn't help, so I clammed up. I don't feel sorry for the little garden gnome very often, but I did then. He was like a puppy someone had abandoned on the median.

He brightened up the next morning, when on the tails of his triumph he was invited by the chairman of the North American Chapter of the International Tomato-Growers Association to deliver the keynote speech at the farewell breakfast. It was a chance for him to emulate one of Nero Wolfe's soliloquys to the suspects in a big-ticket murder case, and if there was one place where his self-appointed protégé surpassed his mentor, it was pomposity.

He spoke forty-five minutes nonstop. Just as he turned away from the podium, a delegate from the Wisconsin branch of the Esteemed Vine (I don't make up this drivel) rose from the audience to ask how Lyon had come to suspect the blue tomato was a fake.

"Admiral Rumple scorned our revered Herbert Lydecker as nothing more than a rough carpenter," Lyon said, "but for all his twenty-first-century expertise, he'd have benefited from a lesson in elementary photography. Lighting is every bit as important as composition. When I first made the acquaintance of *Lycopersicum rumplicus*, it was early evening, and the shadows on the fruit were commensurate with the time of day: They were opposite the source of light, which was right and proper. Yesterday morning, however, when the rays of the sun were shining through the east windows, the shadows had not moved. Had the object in the case been solid, they would then have been on the side opposite the windows; but they were not. In twelve hours they had not moved an iota."

The occupants of the packed gallery rose to their feet, pounding their palms. It would have been a good moment to sit down, but the sawed-off ham was warming up all over again. He raised his hands and pushed his palms toward the crowd, waving them back into their seats.

"Before we adjourn," he said, "I should like to share with you an amusing anecdote from our nation's infancy, when a traitor in President Washington's domestic staff sought to poison him by feeding him tomatoes, which as of course we all know were thought at the time to be poisonous. It seems—"

I stood up and blasted my whistle in his ear. "Train!"

SNAKES AND THE FAT MAN: THE CASE OF NERO WOLFE

The following—with some late emendations—is the introduction I wrote for the 1992 Bantam Books reissue of *Fer-de-Lance*, Nero Wolfe's inaugural adventure, as it was written and submitted before editorial excisions were made. This is its first appearance in the form in which it was composed.

Series are seldom read in order. By the time the average reader discovers a continuing character the chronicle is usually well advanced, and except in the case of those dreary series whose titles are numbered prominently on the covers (to avoid confusion among the interchangeable plots), he has no way of knowing at what point in the saga the book he has just acquired takes place. This can cause distress, particularly if the *next* book he reads is an earlier entry in which the hero he knows as widowed appears with his wife, or having quit smoking and drinking, is seen puffing and guzzling happily away with no explanation for his relapse.

Rex Stout avoided this situation through the simple expedient of never changing his characters.

The Nero Wolfe and Archie Goodwin of *A Family Affair*, the forty-sixth (and last) book in the epoch of West Thirty-Fifth Street, are essentially the same thought-and-action team we met forty-two years earlier in *Fer-de-Lance*. And therein lies the secret of the magic.

Under the present technocracy, when even the nine-to-five ethic has come to seem medieval, we can find peace in the almost Edwardian order of life in the old brownstone: Plant rooms, nine to eleven A.M. and four to six P.M.; office, eleven A.M. to one fifteen P.M.; six P.M. to dinnertime (and after dinner if necessary), day in and day out, except Sunday. Like Holmes's corpulent brother Mycroft—an uncle, perhaps? Stout is coy on this point—Wolfe "has his rails and he runs on them." Nothing short of a major catastrophe, such as a submachine gun assault on the plant rooms (*The Second Confession*), can persuade him to alter that comfortable routine or, worse, leave home on business. Barring extreme circumstances, he will be found in those places at those hours in 1976 and 1934 and all the years between with all his virtues and vices intact. One wishes that family values and the U.S. dollar were to remain as stable.

The reader new to Wolfe and Goodwin may be surprised upon reading *Fer-de-Lance* to learn that it represents their debut. So many references are made to earlier adventures in such an offhand, familiar way by narrator Archie, and his abrasive relationship with his eccentric employer fits them so much like a beloved and well-worn suit of clothes, that the newcomer may be excused the assumption that he has encountered the canon in midstride. Throughout the book, and indeed throughout the series, the sense is acute that these two fixed planets and their satellites—laconic Theodore Horstmann, keeper of the orchids and protector of the faith, Fritz Brenner, the unflappable cook and major-domo, loyal and efficient bloodhounds Saul Panzer, Fred Durkin, and (sometimes) Orrie Cather, and the volcanic Inspector LT Cramer—exist beyond the margins of the page and that their lives do not start and stop with the first and last chapters. Has any other saga begun with a statement as casual as "There was no reason why I shouldn't have been sent for the beer that day . . ."?

When *Fer-de-Lance* appeared, popular crime literature was divided between the manorial "English School" of puzzle mysteries and the two-fisted American urban variety that took its inspiration from the headlines of Prohibition and Depression. Now, more than eight decades later, that division still exists, but there is evidence that the two camps are drifting closer together as both the grim butler and the sadistic bootlegger fade further into history. From the start, Stout wedded the forms. Nero Wolfe, the eccentric genius swathed in his one-seventh of a ton, is a combination Sherlock Holmes in his more contemplative moments and Baroness Orczy's sedentary Old Man in the Corner, while Archie Goodwin exemplifies the hardboiled, wisecracking "private dick" prevalent in pulp fiction. Consider this exchange:

WOLFE: "Your errand at White Plains was in essence a primitive business enterprise: an offer to exchange something for something else. If Mr. Anderson had only been there he would probably have seen it so. It may yet materialize; it is still worth some small effort. I believe though it is getting ready to rain."

GOODWIN: "It was clouding up as I came in. Is it going to rain all over your clues?"

WOLFE: "Someday, Archie, when I decide you are no longer worth tolerating, you will have to marry a woman of very modest mental capacity to get an appreciative audience for your wretched sarcasms."

Not exactly the Holmes-Watson relationship, but a symbiotic one. Without Goodwin's badgering, Wolfe would certainly starve, collapsing under the weight of his own sloth. Without Wolfe—well, we learn from *In the Best Families* that Goodwin can get along only too well without any oddball geniuses around to coddle, but we may assume by how readily he takes up his old post when Wolfe returns from his enforced sabbatical that for all Archie's grousing he prefers the status quo, as do we.

We read Nero Wolfe because we like a good mystery. We *re-*read him not for the plots, which lack the human complexity of Raymond Chandler's or the ingenuity of Agatha Christie's, but for the chemistry between the orchid-fancying enfant terrible and his optimistic-cynical amanuensis and all-around dogsbody, and for the insular complacency of life in the venerable townhouse where world-class meals are served three times daily, the *Cattleyas Laelias* continue to get on splendidly with the *Laeliocattleya Lustre*, and a peek through the tricked-up waterfall picture in Wolfe's office may provide a glimpse of the Great Man relaxing in his custom-built chair with some arcane volume, or pushing his lips in and out with his eyes closed over some dense pattern of facts, while his legman sits by the telephone, waiting for his cue to gather all the suspects and other interested parties for the denouement. It is a world where all things make sense in time, a world better than our own. If you are an old hand making a return swing through its orbit, welcome back; pull up the red leather chair and sit down. If this is your first trip, I envy you the surprises that await you behind that unprepossessing front door.

Oh—about the snake. You didn't think I was going to spoil *that*, did you?

RECOMMENDED READING

Baring-Gould, William S. *Nero Wolfe of West Thirty-Fifth Street*. New York: Viking, 1969. Baring-Gould, to all intents and purposes, invented the biography of characters of fiction with his seminal *Sherlock Holmes of Baker Street*. His is the first serious attempt to gather the sly hints and offhand comments supplied by Archie Goodwin into a coherent account of their partnership.

Darby, Ken. *The Brownstone House of Nero Wolfe*. New York: Little, Brown, 1983. Purporting to be an architectural "life" of the premises in which Wolfe and Goodwin began all their adventures, Darby's book undertakes to solve the conundrum of the many discrepancies in Archie's accounts, seasoning their exploits with arch commentary along the way.

Goldsborough, Robert. *Death on Deadline*. New York: Bantam, 1987. Those who have exhausted the Stout canon and crave more could do a good deal worse than Goldsborough, who captures the tone and cadence of the originals as well as can be done. However, I counsel readers *not* to approach this first in the extended series until they've read *A Family Affair*, Stout's last Wolfe, as he commits the cardinal sin of giving away the identity of the murderer in that book; something his predecessor never did.

Lescroart, John T. *Son of Holmes*. New York: Donald I. Fine, 1986. Lescroart has moved on from the ghetto of the midlist writer to bestsellerdom, and well served; but this early work has a special place in my heart. The title flushes Stout out from the cover of his sly hints about Wolfe's parentage, and the densest flatfoot in Lieutenant Cramer's detail would draw a straight line from Nero Wolfe to Lescroart's "Auguste Lupa." This affectionate tribute is so winning, one almost regrets the stunning success that prevented the author from continuing the series.

Steinbrunner, Chris, and Otto Penzler. *Encyclopedia of Mystery & Detection*. New York: McGraw-Hill, 1976. Pages 426–429 provide a valuable primer and "CliffsNotes" introduction to Archie's prose edda, chronicling the principals' professional and personal characters in detail, and including all of Wolfe's appearances on film, radio, and television to date of publication.

Stout, Rex. The Nero Wolfe series, of course; any edition. It's still in print and always will be. Start with *Fer-de-Lance* (1934) and read straight through *A Family Affair* (1975).

Stout, Rex. *The Nero Wolfe Cookbook*. New York: Viking, 1973. With the help of his editors, Wolfe's creator provides mouth-watering details to aid the ambitious cook in replicating the sumptuous dishes referred to throughout the canon. This is to be recommended to mystery aficionados and amateur chefs alike.

Symons, Julian. *Great Detectives: Seven Original Investigations*. New York: Abrams, 1981. I was privileged to have spent a jolly couple of hours boating down the Thames, courtesy of our mutual British publisher, with Symons, and to enjoy his wit and erudition on all things, the mystery included. So it was with great pleasure I obtained and read this tongue-in-cheek collection of "interviews" with crime fiction's most celebrated sleuths. Symons's "session" with

Archie Goodwin, comfortably retired with his wife, the former Lily Rowan, clears the muddy record, and provides a tantalizing answer to the question of what became of Nero Wolfe after he departed the fabled brownstone.

Winn, Dilys. *Murder Ink: The Mystery Reader's Companion.* New York: Workman, 1977. Winn's is a spine-tingling (and toe-warming) *hommage* to the best of mystery fiction from Day One. Although I take issue with its cynical evaluation of "overrated" entries in the rich world of melodramatic mayhem (the book is, after all, aimed toward wide-eyed readers new to the genre as well as veterans), self-described private investigator Anthony Spiesman's "Nero Wolfe Consultation" provides a delightful visit to the Great Man's storied office.

ACKNOWLEDGMENTS

I'd like to thank Janet Hutchings, editor-in-chief of *Ellery Queen's Mystery Magazine*, and Otto Penzler for placing Claudius Lyon before the world; also Ben LeRoy and his excellent staff at Tyrus Books for allowing me to collect some of my favorite works between two covers.

COPYRIGHTS